INNOCENT KNOWLEDGE

INNOCENT KNOWLEDGE

MAGGIE OWEN

Library of Congress Control Number:		2017919678
ISBN:	Hardcover	978-1-5434-7509-8
	Softcover	978-1-5434-7511-1
	eBook	978-1-5434-7510-4

Print information available on the last page.

Cover images created by Created by freepik
Created by Rwdd_studios - Freepik.com

Rev. date: 01/09/2018

To order additional copies of this book, contact:
Xlibris
1-888-795-4274
www.Xlibris.com
Orders@Xlibris.com
770786

This book is dedicated to my daughters – Ashlynn and Kaitlynn and my grandchildren – Jadyn, Cassydi and Jeremiah. I will love you all forever.

Special appreciation to John and Mary Lou Crosby for putting up with me for so many years!

CHAPTER 1

Freezing rain had just begun to fall, but Morgan still stood there, getting wet and waiting. She was almost out of money and scared out of her mind, and she was desperately trying to figure out some way to keep her daughters safe and keep herself alive. As well as she could tell, this was her last chance, but she didn't know if her last chance was going to save her or simply hasten her ending. She was not even certain if it mattered to anyone at all.

She was standing on the sidewalk outside the Richard B. Russell Building in Atlanta, Georgia. A few years before, the building had been used exclusively for the Immigration and Naturalization Service. Eventually, though, the need for more office space, more investigators, and a much larger reception area had caused the INS to move to another building in Atlanta. The Federal Bureau of Investigation had taken over the building prior to the Olympics coming to Atlanta. There was also another "secret" building in Atlanta, a large office building in the downtown area of the city presumably used by a large corporation. The offices of this building were actually filled with federal agents planning stakeouts, drug raids, search and seizure operations, and the like. Morgan wasn't supposed to know this. But then again, if she hadn't known lots of things she wasn't supposed to know anyway, she wouldn't have been standing outside the federal building in January, with freezing drizzle falling on her.

"Hello, Ms. Jackson," said a voice behind her. Morgan knew who it was, so she didn't bother to turn around.

"Hi," she said. "Are you going to listen to me or arrest me?"

"To be honest, I really haven't decided yet. The Georgia Bureau of Investigation is looking for you, along with a couple of city and county agencies. You're quite a catch. The only problem is, you've piqued my curiosity. If only a third of what you claim to know is true, I could make a huge bust, get promoted, and retire at a relatively early age. You could be a career maker, Ms. Jackson."

Frank Haggarty had a warm, friendly face, but it showed signs of aging well beyond his years. He was an FBI agent who had probably seen more things than he ever imagined he would and a man who had probably lost his wife and family several years earlier due to the long hours he worked. Still he was her last hope and the last one she could even try to trust. Morgan really hoped she wasn't walking into a trap. Everything had gotten so crazy it was impossible for her to tell.

"Ms. Jackson, while I generally enjoy the outdoors, I don't intend to stand out here in the freezing rain with you. Shall we go inside?"

"Mr. Haggarty, while I generally don't enjoy freezing to death outside, I do intend to stay out of that building until I am certain you're not totally biased on their side. Now as far as I can tell, we have two choices: One, we can go for a ride in my car, not yours, and you'll drive while I talk. Two, we can find somewhere to go sit and drink coffee while I talk in a very public place."

"Or three, I can haul you inside right now and make you talk," he said.

"I guess you could, but you don't have any federal charges and no grounds to hold me. I certainly would not tell you anything as you cannot make me say anything. As soon as the good old boys from the GBI show up, you'll have to let me go with them. Then not only have you killed me, you've lost your big chance." Morgan smiled at him and then said, "And to be frank, I'm really almost too tired to care which one happens. I don't have much left to lose, except my daughters. And unless I can remedy this, I've lost them too. Now what would you like to do?"

"Let's start with a ride, Ms. Jackson, and you start talking." Haggarty smiled. Morgan figured since he had given in about the car ride, he'd at least listen for an hour or so.

They walked the two blocks to Morgan's car, and she handed Haggarty her keys. "I'm all yours," Morgan said.

"Just tell me something to make it worth my while. I hate to waste time."

Morgan leaned back in the passenger seat of her car and lit a cigarette. She took a long drag and watched the smoke rise up in the air. She couldn't decide where she wanted to begin, so she finally decided she would start a little before the beginning mainly because she wasn't certain where the real beginning was. Haggarty drove around the block while Morgan contemplated her tale.

"OK, Agent Haggarty, here goes. I divorced my husband while living in Florida. And after growing very weary of custody battles and court cases related to the custody issue, I moved to Williamstown, Georgia. Williamstown is a small community just outside of Clarkston, Georgia. Clarkston is a suburb in Atlanta, which proudly boasts being the home of a large university and a company that is one of the world's largest cable and wire manufacturers. Clarkston is about an hour drive west of Atlanta, but sometimes it seems to be on the other side of the world. But I'm getting well ahead of myself."

"Ms. Jackson, the town history is interesting but hardly a matter of federal security. Could we please continue?"

"You've got to listen, and you've got to understand the whole situation or you won't ever get it. Some of this happened because of my stupidity, and some of it just happened. But there are some people dead, and there are some guys running around killing people, basically at will. And if you'd like to know about it, you've got to listen to understand." Morgan watched his face closely. He didn't show any expression, and she knew he wouldn't—they were taught that in FBI 101. But sometimes you could see their eyes gleam or see their eyes go pitch-black. Black eyes, she had found, were always a very bad sign.

"Please continue, Ms. Jackson, and excuse my impatience. I humbly apologize." Haggarty almost laughed. Morgan assumed he was enjoying being out of the office and probably hoping against hope that she would give him something worthwhile, something he could document.

"I purchased a fairly large home in the only upper-class subdivision in Williamstown on a three-acre lot. Most of the lot was wooded, with a small stream running across the back of the lot to a lake we could use for fishing and swimming. I loved living there and was certain my two daughters would grow up quite well-adjusted and happy, living in this safe small community. Our house was at the end of the cul-de-sac, with only two other houses on the street. The house on our right was occupied, but the house across the cul-de-sac was for sale. A doctor and his girlfriend briefly occupied that house, but after he lost his practice, they had disappeared in the middle of the night. Other than that, it was always quiet and peaceful on our street."

"That's very lovely," Haggarty said. "Used to live somewhere like that myself."

"Another reason I loved living there was it was not far from the day-care center I eventually managed to buy and was less than four miles from the elementary school my daughters would attend. It was also fairly close to my hometown where I had grown up as a little girl. It just felt right being back in Georgia. I thought I had the perfect setup—a business I could run, a job where my children could stay with me after school, a small crime-free town to call home, and still be only an hour away from a major city. I could not have made a more inaccurate assumption, and I doubt I could have ever intentionally put my family in more danger than I did."

"Anyone can make a mistake, Ms. Jackson. Would you mind if I call you, Morgan? First names are so much more personable, don't you think?"

"I really couldn't care less what you call me, Mr. Haggarty," she said.

"Frank, please, Morgan."

"Whatever, Frank." Morgan lit another cigarette and continued, "Part of the process of becoming a licensed day-care owner was to submit fingerprints to the state to be checked for a criminal record. The day-care regulation office provides the paperwork, but one has to go to their local police station to be fingerprinted. I received my form and drove down the road to the police station in Williamstown, which was a three-room building with a secretary and two policemen. One officer, the chief, worked the day shift. And another officer worked the night shift. I asked the secretary who could fingerprint me, and she radioed the chief, who promptly showed up to help.

"The chief, John Henson, looked incredibly old to me but was very friendly and went out of his way to make jokes about fingerprinting me and even helped getting the ink off of my fingers after we had my prints on the proper forms. I told him about the day-care center, and he said he lived right down the road from there and offered to help in any way he could. I thanked him and left, happy to have the fingerprinting done with. I went back to the business of trying to run my day care and didn't think any more about John or the fingerprinting.

"A couple of weeks went by, and one day, John pulled into the driveway of the day-care center. I was outside watching some of the kids play, and he walked over to the fence and waved. I walked over and asked him what was up, and he said he just wanted to check and see how everything was going. He also mentioned he had been a close friend of the man who had owned the house I bought. He said they had been friends for years, and he asked how I had come across the house.

"I thought he was asking a lot of questions, but deciding that he was only trying to make conversation, I gave him an abbreviated version of how I had come to know Lucas Brown and eventually buy his house."

"Wait a minute, Morgan. You know Lucas Brown personally, or you just know of him?" This was the first time Haggarty seemed truly interested in what she had to say.

"Lucas Brown had made a career in law enforcement in Georgia, rapidly rising through the ranks to become the youngest warden in Georgia history. Later he progressed further to head up the SWAT team operations in Georgia. Lucas was in charge of controlling and containing all prison riots in Georgia, handling any hostage situations and the personal security of the lieutenant governor and governor of Georgia. Lucas had a friend who was a Clarkston police detective, and the two of them saw the advantages of opening a private probation company in Clarkston. The two men coupled the probation office with private investigation services and personal security and opened a small company."

"Come on, Morgan. That's pretty good background, but you could have found any of that in the local Clarkston newspaper if you looked long enough. Give me something here. I'm getting bored."

Frank said he was getting bored, but Morgan thought he might have been getting interested. He turned onto I-285 and began the eighty-five-mile circle around Atlanta.

"Just listen a little longer, Frank, and I think you might get interested. If you don't, I'll buy you a cup of coffee and you can hand me over to the Georgia Bureau of Investigation, your GBI, and go home and watch television."

Frank glanced at Morgan with a frown but decided not to say anything, and she continued her tale. "During my custody battle with my ex-husband, threats progressed to a level that was alarming to me. And fearing my ex-husband would try to kidnap the children, I mentioned to a friend that I could use some sort of security. Money was not a problem for me at that particular time, and my friend suggested a gentleman who had installed a surveillance system for him at his business.

"This gentleman was Robert, who just happened to be Lucas Brown's best friend and business partner. I became their second client. Initially, I used their services for protection for my daughters. They would escort us to court hearings and to and from meetings with attorneys. Later they installed a security system in my home in Florida and did some surveillance on my ex-husband. I was always impressed with the work they did, and over the course of several months, we became friends. I bought a boat from Robert and Lucas, and when I told them I was looking for a home in the Clarkston area, Lucas had told me about his house being for sale. That was how I had ended up in Williamstown, and I had told John about a quarter of that story. When I finished my abbreviated version of the story, John just smiled at me and drove off from the day-care center.

"The following weekend, I decided we needed a break, so the girls and I took off for Hilton Head, South Carolina, for a couple of days. We ended up having such a good time that we stayed an extra day. Monday evening, as we were driving down the main street of

Williamstown, I looked in my rearview mirror and saw the blue lights of a police cruiser flashing.

"I pulled over on the shoulder of the road, and the cruiser did also. John appeared from the car and walked up to my window. I asked him what was wrong, and he stood there and said he had missed me and was wondering when I was coming home. I asked how he knew I had gone away, and he told me Williamstown was a small town and everyone knew everything that happened. I told him that I didn't realize my leaving town for a couple of days constituted a happening, and he said I might be surprised what made a happening in Williamstown. Then he welcomed us home and drove away. I didn't have enough sense to know it then, but that was pretty much a happening in itself. He was telling me he was watching, but I didn't know it then.

"One problem I had at the day-care center was that by Georgia law, one could not smoke cigarettes anywhere on a day-care property, not even in the parking lot. Being an avid smoker, this presented somewhat of a problem for me. Eventually, I began driving from the day care to the far end of Williamstown to one of the town's two gas stations. This gave me just enough time to quickly smoke a cigarette during the ride. Once there, I'd buy a cup of coffee from the store and drive back to the center, puffing the whole way. If I drove slowly, the whole trip would take maybe fifteen minutes, but I enjoyed the short breaks, not to mention the boost of caffeine and nicotine."

"You do smoke a lot, Morgan," Frank said, laughing.

"Yeah, well, part of that could be due to you guys, don't you think?"

"Now you've hurt my feelings, Morgan. Do I make you nervous? We're the good guys, remember?"

"That remains to be seen, Frank. No offense, but I haven't had a lot of good luck with any of you guys."

"Morgan, cops are like guys you go out with. Just because you met one that was a dud, it doesn't mean that all guys you date are going to be the same. Seems a shame someone as pretty as you would be so cynical."

She turned and looked at him. She decided not to say anything, rather opted to light yet another cigarette and continue with her story. "Not too long after I began my little gas station trips, John would show up in the station, always buying cigarettes or coffee. We'd exchange pleasantries, and I'd go on my way. Sometimes he'd follow me out into the parking lot and continue our conversation, which mostly consisted of talking about the weather, the day-care center, or the apparent lack of crime in the big city of Williamstown. During one such meeting, John suggested that when I drove through town and saw his police cruiser parked alongside the road, I should stop and visit with him. After all, he said there wasn't too much for him to do in Williamstown. I didn't really think much about it, but stopping alongside the road or in parking lots gave me an excuse to smoke an extra cigarette or two. And pretty soon, we were talking to each other three or four times a day."

"Cigarette smoking can be hazardous to your health, Morgan. Surgeon general says so." Frank laughed again but began cursing as someone cut him off, changing lanes.

"If you're ready, I'll continue, Frank."

"Please do, my lady. I'm all ears."

"I began enjoying these conversations as they became full of the town gossip. I learned all the details of the prim-and-proper citizens of Williamstown, most of whom were not so prim and proper according to John. I learned of affairs, DUI arrests, divorces, bankruptcies, and illegal drug uses.

"I knew who the child molesters were and the bookies. I knew where the local supply of marijuana was grown and where a few bodies had been found. I must admit, I found most of this quite intriguing but mostly as a way of passing time and being curious, I suppose. One day, I had mentioned to John that I had seen his cruiser drive down the road early that morning, around five in the morning, while I was sitting on my back porch, drinking a cup of coffee and smoking, of course. John said he always went to work early, but if I were regularly up at that time of the morning, he'd stop by some morning for a cup of coffee. I felt vaguely strange about the suggestion. But I also was enjoying our conversations, and I figured, who else was safer to have a cup of coffee with than the chief of police? I told him it would be fine. Two days later, at five in the morning sharp, John Henson was knocking on my door.

"This started a ritual that would continue in the same fashion for about six months. Three mornings a week, John would come by my house. And if it wasn't too cold or raining, we'd sit on the porch, drink coffee, and talk. If the weather didn't permit the porch sitting, we'd sit at the kitchen table, but rarely did we stay in the house. I loved these talks as most of my other conversations during the day were with children five years old or younger. John was always the perfect gentleman, and I started thinking of us as genuine friends.

"Occasionally, I would talk to him about my daughters' father and the troubles that evolved out of our divorce. John talked about serving in the marines and how that period of his life had such a lasting effect on him.

"John had enlisted in the marines when he was only nineteen years old. Apparently, he worked very hard and made his way to the special forces. Eventually, he became a sniper and spent a great deal of his time in the military, sneaking through forests or mountains with only a small group of men with him. Usually, according to John, they were on their own and, on more than one occasion, were left totally to their own strategy to escape some very dangerous situations. John was shot and stabbed by a target, and that was the end of his stint in the marines.

"After recovering from his injuries, John said he spent quite a while hitchhiking around the South, not really going anywhere and not really doing anything. He said he finally got tired and went home to his grandmother's. He then applied for and accepted a position with a local police department. Thus began the career in law enforcement."

"Your John has had a pretty lucrative job as a chief from what I hear," Frank said. "How close exactly did the two of you get?"

"Do you know him?" Morgan asked. Part of her wanted to hear something good about John, what a fine officer he was. The other part of her knew what he was. That scared Morgan, and she still didn't want to believe it.

"Morgan, you tell me what you know, and then I'll tell you the parts that I can. I believe, although I might be wrong, you know more about John Henson than I do. I've got to find somewhere for us to pull off. It's starting to snow."

Morgan looked out the window and realized she hadn't even noticed when the rain turned into snow. Snow is a rarity in Atlanta and brings with it the usual havoc of a tornado or a flood. Atlantans are poorly prepared to drive in snow, and usually, the roads are closed due to accidents long before they would ever be closed due to accumulated snow. Three inches of snow in Atlanta would close all schools, most businesses, and most certainly, all roads, highways, or two lanes. Frank was wise to want to get off the interstate.

Morgan looked out the window and fell into a memory. About six months after they had begun talking at Morgan's house, a friend of Morgan's had taken her daughters for the weekend to give Morgan a break. Morgan was appreciative of the "downtime" but had no plans. Since her separation, she had not dated and really had no intention of doing so. Her big plans for the evening were to clean the house and sit down and read a book uninterrupted. Morgan, of course, had told John of the approaching break from motherhood.

Somewhere around midnight that Friday night, her doorbell rang. She had looked through the peephole, wondering who would be there at that time of the night. When she saw it was John, she opened the door, wondering honestly why he was there.

"I need you" was all he said.

He walked in the door and wrapped his arms around her. He kissed her neck, her cheeks, and finally, her lips. Morgan's entire body had tingled. It was the first time he had ever kissed her. Morgan wasn't sure if it was because she trusted him because he had been such a gentleman for so long, because they were friends, or simply because she was lonely. But instead of saying anything, Morgan took his hand and led him upstairs to her bedroom even though she knew instinctively this was wrong.

They made love for hours that night, and eventually, Morgan fell asleep in his arms. The two of them never said a word that night, but Morgan still just could not shake the feeling she had just made a really bad decision. "We became lovers eventually" was what Morgan said to Frank as he pulled into a Holiday Inn restaurant parking lot.

"I figured as much, Morgan. Please tell me this isn't going to be a 'jilted lover' thing. If I listen to you much longer, we're going to get snowed in. And I'll be sitting here with a miffed woman who's wanted, God knows for what, by half the people in Georgia." Frank looked genuinely concerned that Morgan might be making up a case based on jealousy or something along those lines. And for a moment, she wished it was that simple.

They got out of the car and walked into the restaurant. Morgan knew Frank was wondering what she had to say, but she also knew if she didn't present her side just like a sales pitch, he'd never believe her. And she was only going to get one chance at having him listen to her. Morgan decided time would be on her side as long as she gave him just enough to keep him interested. Anyway, it was snowing, and there wasn't too far he could go. Maybe she had finally caught a break. *That would certainly be something new,* Morgan thought.

They went in the restaurant and took a booth in a corner in the back smoking section. To Morgan's delight, Frank pulled a cigarette out of his coat pocket and lit up. It was the first time she had seen him smoke.

"What would you like to eat, Morgan?" he asked. "It's on the government."

"I'm not at all hungry, but I'd love a rum and Coke, thank you," she replied.

"Drinking's not good, dear. It distorts one's memory."

"So does being shot at. So does losing everything. I'm down to drinking or drugs, Frank. Drugs are illegal, so I guess I should stick to the booze, don't you think?"

"Are you always so direct, Morgan? I checked on you, you know. No record, no speeding tickets, nothing. Not until now, and now you've got the whole state looking for you. And I'm really not sure why. What the hell did you do?"

"I didn't do anything intentionally. I think I got a couple of people killed, though. I didn't know. I thought it was all OK. Everyone was the police. All these guys were supposed to be good. I used to really believe that."

"Morgan, I'm going to order dinner, and you can have one drink. But you better get moving on this story. We're getting snowed in, and you're running out of time."

Being a true Southern gentleman, Frank ordered his meal and her drink. They didn't talk much until the waitress had served his food. Morgan gulped her drink and ordered another. Morgan assumed Frank figured that if she loosened up, she was to come closer to telling the truth. But Morgan was telling the truth, or at least the truth as she knew it to be, so she wasn't worried about drinking. Morgan wasn't worried about anything, except she wanted to go home to a home she no longer had and to children she didn't know if she would see anymore. She wasn't worried at all about having a couple of drinks. No problem there.

CHAPTER 2

Frank began eating his dinner, and while she smoked another cigarette and sipped her second drink, she watched the snowfall through the window. The Atlanta skyline was obscured by the gray sky. There was nothing to see, except the large snowflakes falling to the concrete. Morgan liked that—the weather seemed to match how she felt. Morgan sat there and wondered how she could ever have gotten in this situation. Still she silently drank her drink and stared out the window.

"So tell me, Morgan," said Frank with a large mouthful of steak. "What else do you know about John Henson?"

"I don't know much except what John told me, but he told me a lot. How much is true, I have no idea. Some of it's factual because I found stories in the newspapers. Some of it, I don't guess I'll ever know if it's true or not." Morgan shrugged. She really didn't know and really didn't know what else to say.

"OK, go on. You and John were lovers. I can see why he was attracted to you, but this still doesn't make a federal case."

Morgan ordered a third drink, ignored Frank's scowl, and continued with her story. "We began seeing each other, intimately, a couple of times a week. He'd always come over around three or four in the morning, stay a couple of hours, and leave. It was kind of weird. But I was busy running the day-care center and didn't want my kids to know what we were doing, so l guess it worked.

"Anyway, somewhere around this time, a friend of mine had purchased the skating rink in town and needed an investor for operating capital. Now what I knew about skating rinks, you could put in your shirt pocket. But I liked kids, obviously, and l figured it might be fun. Two months into the deal, my friend couldn't make the payments and started skimming money from the rink. She was just really hard up for money, but I didn't want to throw any more money into the business without getting a return. And a month or so later, she simply signed the rink over to me in lieu of the money she had borrowed.

"By now, the skating rink was in pretty bad shape. But I cut the expenses as much as I could and started having all kinds of special events, and it turned around. Everything started working quite well. Anyway, one thing we started doing was having what was called soul night at the rink. I brought in a black disc jockey, and that one night a week, only soul music and rap were played. Danny, the disc jockey, was a bit of a sleaze. But he brought in his security guys, and the black townspeople flocked to see him narrate the show. They skated for four hours, and the last hour, they danced. It was really a cool thing, and all in all, the huge crowd was always very mannerly. Once in a while, some of the guys would go out in the parking lot and drink a couple beers in their cars. But other than that, there wasn't a problem. This one weekly event dug the little skating rink out of a financial mess.

"So everything was rolling along all right, except John started complaining about not seeing me enough. See, from five thirty in the morning until four in the afternoon, I worked at the day care—except for smoke breaks—and then I went straight to the skating rink and worked until midnight or later."

"Didn't leave too much time for socializing, did it, Morgan?" Frank shook his head disapprovingly. "You know, too much work isn't healthy, honey."

Morgan ignored that and continued with the story. "About this time, John decided he could fill in for some of the security guards on his days off. His logic was, he could use the extra money and we could spend some time together. I thought it might be useful to have someone I knew I could trust working there, and I didn't particularly care whom I paid the security money to, so I agreed. We scheduled his first night at work to be the next soul night, the first Sunday in August.

"The night started like all the other soul nights. Danny came in early and set up his equipment. The security guards all took their places, and John was in the office with me to protect the money and keep me safe, so he said. The people started flowing in, and with them came the money. Around ten that night, I had finished wrapping up the money, and John walked around the rink with me while I checked the skate room, concession stand, and restrooms.

"All of a sudden, somebody came running through the front, screaming that someone was coming in with a gun and someone had been shot outside. It was the damnedest thing I'd ever seen. The music stopped, and like a stampede, they ran through the door, screaming and yelling. Even Danny took off, leaving his sound equipment and all behind. The next thing I knew, the Clarkston police were at the end of the driveway that led down to the rink and had it blocked off. Nobody could get in or out, and everybody was going crazy. John told me to go in the office and wait and he'd go see what had happened."

"So what had happened?"

"Well, John walked up the hill and stayed for about an hour. From the front doors, I could see John talking to the cops, but they were too far away for me to hear them. Anyway, about an hour later, John came back and said there had been a gang-related shooting about half a block away from the rink. He said the cops figured the person who came running in the rink was actually the person who had fired the gun. But no one seemed to know who this guy was, and they were still looking for him. John started laughing and said everything was all right and for me to go home and not worry. He said it didn't have anything to do with the rink. He said it was no big deal. I never knew if he really believed that or if it was just another big lie. Maybe he really thought he could fix the problem. I don't know."

"So the guy who fired the shot turned out to be a problem for you, Morgan?"

"Yeah, turned out to be a big problem. The next morning, the chief of police from Clarkston called me at the day-care center and asked me to come down to his office. I went down there and was told to close my skating rink. When I asked him why, he said the rink wasn't the kind of establishment that was wanted in Clarkston. I told him it was my understanding that the shooting had occurred away from the rink and that none of the participants had ever been to the rink, at least not until after the shooting had occurred. He said it didn't matter. He wanted me to close."

Frank looked puzzled and raised his eyebrows. Morgan liked his eyes. They sometimes softened, like deep down, maybe he believed her even though he didn't have any reason to believe anything she said.

"I couldn't get anywhere with the man. I even knew him, knew he had invested in Robert and Lucas's business as a silent partner. That, by the way, was illegal, which was why he was a silent partner. But that's not pertinent here. Anyway, I went to InterSecure to look for Robert to see if he could help. Robert wasn't there, but Lucas was, so I talked to him instead. I told Lucas what had happened, and he hugged me, told me not to worry, and said he'd take care of everything. Lucas said there was no way anyone could make me shut down."

"So Lucas helped you?"

"Well, he said he would. But in the twenty minutes it took me to get from Lucas's office back to Williamstown and find John to talk to him, Lucas had already called John, and John was furious at me."

"OK, Morgan. Now you've lost me," said Frank.

"John said Lucas had called him, raising hell about him being at the rink. He said Lucas offered him a job out of state and wanted John to move immediately. I didn't understand any of that. But I knew I wasn't going to talk to Lucas anymore, and I knew that John was upset. I just didn't know why. Guess that's where being a little country girl from Georgia was detrimental to my well-being."

Morgan smiled as she said the last part, and Frank grinned back. She ordered another drink and watched it snow some more. Morgan didn't know it at the time, but while she was sitting in the restaurant, telling Frank her life story, John and Lucas were having a conversation of their own. Unfortunately for John, though, the conversation wasn't going very well.

"You idiot!" Lucas yelled. "All you had to do was watch her, scare her away if you needed to. And what did you do? You kept her here! Damn it all! You fell in love with her, right?"

"Go to hell, Brown. I'm ashamed of what I did to her and a bunch of other people. I'm tired, Lucas. I just don't give a damn anymore. I don't want to be a part of it anymore."

"I don't think you need to worry about that, John. But what you better worry about is how much you told her. We can't find her."

"Leave her alone, Lucas. She won't talk to anyone, and if she did, who's going to believe her? She doesn't even know what went on."

"What did you tell her?" Lucas turned around. John was actually amused to see his old friend so rattled. Lucas's face was red; his veins were bulging in his forehead, and he was sweating profusely. John had to suppress a grin. Almost instantly, Lucas collected himself and began speaking calmly. He stared at John and carefully chose his words. "John, we've been friends for a long time. Now I can help you, and you can help me, but I've got to know what you told her. We've got to find her, and she's got to be rid of. You know how this works. This isn't about you and her or even you or me. The lives of a lot of men are at stake here. You *know* what's at stake. Help me, John, so I can help you." Lucas finished speaking and turned his back to his friend.

John couldn't help himself any longer. He started laughing. He laughed so long he began to cry. This infuriated Lucas, but he remained silent. Finally, John was able to catch his breath and began talking. "My friend, have you ever thought about how insane all of this has been? This began forty-eight years ago. You'd think it would stop, that at some point in time, it would be over with. How many lives are you going to ruin to cover this up? How many people are you going to send to jail, threaten, and kill before it stops? Morgan might be a pain in the ass, but she's hardly a threat to the United States of America. This is not a national crisis, Lucas. You really need to get a grip here, maybe take a vacation. I'm leaving. I'm through with this. I'm too old to keep this up and don't have the heart for it anymore. I sold my soul a long time ago, and somehow, Morgan gave me a piece of it back. She's so understanding and nonjudgmental. She knows just about everything, Lucas, but she won't be a problem."

Lucas listened intently to John talking, but he never turned to face his friend. Instead, he slowly reached inside his coat pocket and gripped his .45 revolver. He didn't want to kill his friend, but a plan was coming together, and John was sounding like nothing but an old fool. It was probably better this way.

"Lucas, if you try to hurt her again or take her kids away from her, I swear, I'll kill you. It's time for this to stop. It's over. Let it be."

Lucas, still with his back turned, agreed. "You're right, John. It needs to end now." And with that, Lucas swung around, aimed the gun at John's forehead, and shot his friend of thirty years between the eyes.

CHAPTER 3

Morgan sat there and watched Frank scarf down the last bit of his apple pie, which was smothered with vanilla ice cream. Apparently, the man didn't get a good meal very often. Morgan wasn't sure a meal from a hotel restaurant and lounge qualified as such, but who was she to judge? Anyway, Morgan ordered her fourth drink and decided it was good enough for her. As the waitress brought her drink and Frank's coffee, his pager went off, and he politely excused himself to go make a call, reminding Morgan not to leave in his absence.

"I came to you for help, remember? Where do you think I'm going?"

He called her a smart-ass and walked away, grinning.

Twenty minutes passed, and Frank was still gone. Morgan had to use the restroom and decided she couldn't wait until he returned. As she walked across the lounge and down the hallway to the restrooms, Frank came tearing around the corner and grabbed her arm. "Come on, we've got to go. I've got to get you out of here." He had his left hand wrapped around her arm and his right on his holster, seemingly ready to pull out his revolver.

"What's wrong? What was the phone call about?" Morgan asked.

"There's a warrant for you now, and everybody is after you. You just might be telling the truth, Morgan. Now wait here till I get the car." He left her standing inside the door and ran to the parking lot. They had been in the restaurant for a couple of hours, and the snow had begun to pile up pretty well. Frank drove the car to the restaurant entrance, and as he did, the rear of the car skidded around. "The parking lot has frozen. I guess that rain you enjoyed standing in this morning has frozen under the snow. We're not going to get very far in this at all," said Frank as he slowly maneuvered the car out of the lot. The streets were rather congested, but it wasn't traffic, just abandoned cars where Atlanta motorists had skidded to untimely stops when the snow had started.

"Are you going to tell me what's wrong and where we're going? What was the phone call about?" Morgan was getting really nervous, and with the snow, she wouldn't have much of a chance to escape anywhere if it became necessary.

"They've got an arrest warrant for you now, Morgan. About an hour ago, your buddy John was shot between the eyes. GBI says your fingerprints are all over the place. They've asked the FBI for assistance in locating you. I'd haul your butt over there except for one thing…"

"I'm innocent or it's snowing?"

"Neither one. An hour ago and a couple of hours before that, you were with me. Now unless you can be in two places at once, you didn't shoot your lover. I believe you might be framed, Ms. Morgan."

"Well, at least this time, I've got an airtight alibi, right?"

"Alibi, yes, but if I take you in while I'm giving my version of events, you'll be transferred back to Clarkston for questioning. And I don't think you'll be very safe."

"I suppose this warrant is for murder, huh?"

"Yeah, Morgan. John is dead. I really am sorry about that, for your sake."

Morgan didn't really know if what she felt was sorrow, relief, or some strange mixture of the two. She knew good and damned well John had done a lot of really awful things. She knew he had caused her a tremendous amount of problems. Despite that, at one time, he had not only been her lover but also her very best friend. He had known everything about her—all her secrets, her desires, and her dreams. Morgan thought she had always assumed at some point that they would be able to sit down and talk, at least one last time, so she could understand what had happened. Morgan didn't say anything. She didn't have anything left to say.

Everything seemed so hopeless, and she wasn't naive enough to believe Frank was really going out of his way to help. People just generally don't do that, and now that the warrant was issued, Frank was actually required to take her into custody. Morgan looked out the window at the sky. The sun had all but disappeared, and there was nothing to see but gray clouds and falling snowflakes. They were moving slowly in the traffic, and soon Frank was muttering about people who didn't know how to drive in the snow.

Actually, most of the problem stemmed from Atlanta not being prepared for snow. There were precious few trucks to distribute sand and salt on the highways, not to mention the secondary roads. Unless one lived in the North Georgia Mountains, snow chains for one's tires were considered an unnecessary, useless expense—until the one time every five years or so that the central portion of Georgia inches of snow. More often than not, all schools were closed immediately for the next two days, followed closely by most businesses. The entire middle and upper portions of the state generally closed down for a day or two when Atlanta had a blizzard. It seemed this snowstorm was going to accomplish much of the same.

"OK, Morgan. We've got to find somewhere to put you for the night, and you've got to tell me everything you know right now."

"I don't even know where I left off. I'm tired, and I really need some sleep. Just drop me off somewhere, and I'll catch a bus."

"That's brilliant. Just how far do you think you're going to get? I want to help you, I really do, but we don't have much time to figure this out. Can we get to your kids?"

"I'm not about to tell you where my kids are."

"They'll find them, Morgan."

"Not as long as they do what they're supposed to be doing. I'm not going to call them, and I'm sure as hell not going to tell you where they are! Where are we going?" Morgan was starting to panic. She knew John could have very well been responsible for all this. But she also knew, or more precisely "felt," that if John had been murdered, whoever killed him would certainly come after her. She couldn't think clearly. She couldn't think of what she needed to do. She knew the odds were fairly high that Frank was going to drive her straight to the Fulton County Jail.

The heater blew diligently in the car, but Morgan was freezing and having a hard time breathing. A million thoughts streamed through her head, none very useful. She felt physically ill. Morgan knew she was going to vomit if she wasn't out of the car soon. "Frank, I've got to get out. Please just pull over!"

"You've got to get ahold of yourself. Now just calm down. We're almost there."

"Where in the heck is there?"

"My house, Morgan. We're going to my house—the last place they would look. We're going to figure this out, and you're going to tell me everything, truthfully, 'cause I'm sticking my neck way out here." Frank's face was emotionless. Morgan couldn't read it, couldn't tell what he had in mind. His eyes, which she had liked so much earlier because of their gleam, were glassy looking. He was obviously deep in thought, but she couldn't tell how much of his concentration was on the roads and how much was on her. Part of Morgan was convinced that if she ever walked into his home or wherever they were really going, she would never come out alive. Another part of her was convinced that he was still her hope for salvation. Morgan couldn't decide anything, so she did nothing and silently sat there and tried to remember the roads they were turning on.

Ten minutes later, they turned into a driveway of a house in a middle class–looking subdivision. *Probably a three-bedroom, two-bath, split-level plan just like every other house on the block,* thought Morgan. It was rather difficult to tell, though, because of the snow and the overcast sky. Also the sun had set, and the clouds concealed the moon, so it was rather dark.

Frank pulled into the garage, and the automatic door closed behind them. "Come on in, Morgan. It's home for tonight anyway," he said and hopped out of the car with a grin on his face. The house was about what Morgan had pictured but very sparsely furnished. Family pictures hung on the wall of Frank and his wife and children, Morgan assumed, but no one ran to greet him at the door. There was a worn sofa and small television in the living room but no other furnishings. It was strangely bare.

Frank took his overcoat off and threw it across the sofa. "Would you like a cup of coffee? I've got some instant here somewhere…" And for a minute, his mind seemed to wander.

"Hey, Frank. Where's your wife?"

"She's not here anymore. Kids aren't either. She took the furniture, the kids, and the savings. I suppose she would've taken the house, too, except she hated Atlanta and my job. I guess she wasn't ever happy here. Who knows?" He shrugged and headed into his kitchen.

Morgan sat on the edge of the sofa and listened. She could hear pots banging around and some mumbled profanities as something in the kitchen spilled on the floor. It seemed that Frank didn't often entertain in his home. Morgan found it quite calming, though, because she didn't figure that if he was going to kill her or deliver her over to someone who would kill her, he would care whether she had a cup of coffee or not. Simple things can be rather reassuring in times of great stress. Morgan was learning to find great comfort in some of the simplest things of life.

Eventually, Frank emerged with a cup of coffee and a rather proud look on his face. Politely he handed the cup to Morgan and sat down on the far end of the sofa, his face suddenly growing serious and concerned. "All right, Morgan. We have maybe until the morning to work most of this out. The murder charge won't be a problem because you were with me, but what happens between now and getting the charges dropped is a whole different matter. Tell me everything you can think of no matter how unimportant it might seem to you."

CHAPTER 4

While Morgan was sitting on Frank's sofa, trying to remember all she had been told, Lucas was pouring a drink of Crown Royal. He was standing by the bar in his living room. Lucas's house, by all accounts, was a miniature mansion by Clarkston standards—five bedrooms, three baths, living room, formal dining room, and a den he used as an office. The kitchen was state-of-the-art, with more appliances than his wife would ever use, not that she cooked anyway. Most nights, like tonight, she and the kid, Lucas's son, weren't even home. *That was probably best too,* Lucas thought, as he couldn't stand the sight of her. The only reason he'd remained married to her was it would damage his image in town to be divorced again. The last divorce had caused enough problems. He didn't want to go through that again.

He sat in his recliner and stared at his fireplace. There weren't any sounds, except for the logs crackling and popping and the ice cubes rattling in his glass as he sipped his drink. John had lost his edge. That seemed to be happening a lot lately. All the old-timers were getting a conscience. Lucas didn't understand that because these men had been trained for years to do what they did. They killed when necessary, and that was all there was to it. Lucas couldn't see the problem. Maybe these guys were starting to worry about their mortality. Who the hell knew? Surely, these men, who had each killed at least a dozen people in their lifetime, weren't worried about growing old, dying, and having to answer to a higher power. How could any of them possibly seriously believe there was a god when the world was like it was? People stole, murdered, and survived or died. It was just that simple.

Lucas attended church regularly. Every Sunday, Lucas, his wife, and son attended both Sunday school and the morning worship service. Sometimes they even returned in the evenings for the night service. It created a good image—the perfect family, a hardworking, churchgoing family. How could he ever be under scrutiny? He—the perfect small-town citizen, business owner, and church member. *Hell, I might even become a church deacon next year,* mused Lucas.

Then Lucas's face clouded over. He was the least concerned about killing his friend. After all, that was business, and Morgan was going to take the rap for that one anyway. She'd be caught by tomorrow morning, and then she could be disposed of while trying to escape. Lots of murderers run when they know they have no way out, and sometimes accidents were unavoidable. Things happen.

Lucas was concerned about the last informative thing John had said, though. "She knows just about everything" were John's words. How much exactly was "just about everything," and why in the hell would John have done that? *She must've been a good lover,* thought Lucas. But there wasn't a woman on the earth worth dying over, though that was what John had done. He threw away thirty-seven years of a career, the last five of which all he had to do was use his position to cover up a few incidental matters in Clarke County. It should have been a piece of cake, but John had made poor decisions. *No, no remorse here. John got what he deserved. He had gotten careless.* Lucas threw his glass at the fireplace where it shattered. *How much is "just about everything"? Morgan must be disposed of quickly. Where in the hell is she?*

CHAPTER 5

Frank found an ashtray and set it between the two of them on the sofa and told Morgan to start talking.

"OK, remember when I told you about the guy that got shot down the street from the skating rink? Well, a couple of days later, there was a drive-by shooting in Clarkston that was supposedly retaliation for that shooting. According to the paper, the police claimed it was all gang related, and they imposed a 'nine in the evening' curfew for all kids under eighteen. That wasn't real conducive to the skating rink business because the kids didn't want to pay to skate for a couple of hours just to have to turn around and go home. It really sucked. I couldn't have any more soul nights because Danny, the disc jockey, was being harassed by the cops. They had told him not to come back down to the rink or they'd bust him for some sort of drug-related activity. Generally, the police cut the skating business down to a Saturday-and Sunday-afternoon business. It really sucked.

"Anyway, one day, I was complaining to John about the lack of business at the rink. All of a sudden, he declared he was going to retire from the city of Williamstown and come work for me full-time. His argument was that with his reputation, we'd get the business back, and all would be well. I agreed to hire him full-time, and it was the worst decision I ever made in my life.

"John turned in a month's notice to the city, and all hell broke loose. Lucas was on the phone, calling and telling me I didn't want to hire John. It just wouldn't look good, you know. Later that day, I saw Lucas's car parked beside John's police cruiser, and they seemed to be arguing. I don't know what went on. John never told me, but Lucas didn't look very pleased sitting in his car.

"Anyway, John worked out his notice, and we planned a couple of special events at the rink to try to get the kids back. We opened early on Friday night and let the kids in free. The concession stand's income tripled because the kids came in with more money left to spend since they didn't have to pay admission. Families with younger kids started coming out on Fridays. They could skate for free, and the curfew didn't apply to them, so it all worked. Saturday mornings, we'd dress employees in costumes, like Barney the Dinosaur and Mickey Mouse and stuff like that. We started doing really good. Then the fire marshal crap started.

"One Friday night, around ten or so, here comes the county fire inspector. He walked into the rink and wrote down a couple of supposed fire code violations and said I had to close until the items were fixed. It was stupid stuff, like one fire extinguisher's inspection tag had fallen off. It might have been a technical violation, but it sure wasn't worth shutting me down. They ran everybody out of the rink, and we closed. I had the things fixed the very next morning, but it took five more days before the inspector could find time to come back out and say I could reopen. We were open for about a week, and they came back and did the same thing again. We were closed for two weeks the second time."

"Sounds like they were roughing you up, Morgan, but how come? That's what I need to know."

"I don't know, but I knew during this time that John and I spent a lot of time just sitting down at the rink, talking. He seemed to talk a lot about the war and—"

Frank cut her off. "The Vietnam War?"

"Yeah, and some of the people he said he had killed because of things they had done during the war. I mean, he just went on about this stuff for hours. He told me about the first Vietnam vet he killed—a veteran who constantly spoke about his first kill during the Vietnam conflict. The soldier obviously was severely conflicted about his experience and frequently told anyone who would listen what had happened. He said he was checking out a hut in an abandoned village when he heard a noise below him. He looked around on the ground and found the entrance to a tunnel. He said he started firing in the hole. When he went in the tunnel, he found a young woman, around nineteen or twenty years old. His bullet had hit her in the side of her face. She was dead, and she was holding a hand grenade. The vet said he would never forget how her face looked."

Morgan frequently wondered if the man had still been thinking about the young woman when faced with his own mortality. Obviously, Morgan would never know the answer.

"What else did John talk about?"

"Well, he had dozens of stories about stuff like that, and then one day, he got on all the Kennedy assassination crap. He got really quiet one night and, just out of the blue, started with a long tale about the Kennedys, the Koreans, and the CIA and all these deals that had supposedly been made and why Kennedy was killed."

"Morgan, you've got to tell me every single thing you remember about that. This might be the problem."

"You've got to be kidding! This is just all ridiculous stuff that happened, what, more than fifty years ago? I wasn't even born when Kennedy was shot. All I know about it is what I learned in school about what a popular president he was and how shocked the country was when he was killed—"

"And what John told you. Come on, think!" Frank interrupted.

Morgan stood up from the sofa and stretched. She was tired and really just wanted to go to sleep, but she knew that wasn't about to happen. She walked over the window and looked outside. There was nothing to see, except the snow still falling in front of the glow from a streetlamp. Other than that, it was pitch-black. The snow had slowed down considerably, but it was still falling. The city would be shut tomorrow for sure—no school for the kids and no work for most of the parents. Tomorrow would be a lost day.

Morgan told Frank that she really would like a hot shower. He looked annoyed and said they needed to keep talking, but when she told him she was going to fall asleep if she sat there any longer, he relented and pointed her down the hall to his guest bathroom. She had to scrounge around to find a towel, and Frank hung a robe outside the bathroom door. Morgan assumed it used to be his wife's, but it was a thick terry-cloth robe and looked really warm. She wasn't opposed to wearing used clothing, especially if the clothes were warm and cuddly. There was something comforting about soft, cuddly clothes, and by this time, Morgan could use some comforting.

Morgan turned the shower on and let the water start steaming before she stepped inside. It felt wonderful. Her joints ached from being wet and cold that morning in the rain. She hadn't really slept in several days, and every muscle in her body was sore from tension and stress. As the water ran down her back and over her leg, she remembered the night John told her about the Kennedy assassination.

They had been on the sofa in her office at the skating rink. Her daughters were at a friend's house, and they had made love earlier—or at least what Morgan considered making love to be—on the couch. The rink was closed, so there wasn't any danger of anyone coming inside. She had brought them each a cup of coffee, and they were sitting there, not saying much of anything. All at once, John asked her what she knew about the Kennedy plot. Morgan told him she didn't know anything much at all as it was before her time. Really, she didn't care. Not meaning to be unpatriotic or anything, but sometimes old stories grow old and she just couldn't see any relevance to the Kennedys and the two of them sitting in a shut-down skating rink. After all, the government had stated all along that Oswald had shot Kennedy and Jack Ruby had shot Oswald. Case closed.

John had gotten quiet after that. His head was bent down, and he had seemed lost in some deep thought. His eyes were almost shut, just little slits showing, and his forehead had been wrinkled. Deep creases ran across his brow, making him look much older than his fifty-five years. Sometimes John had looked like he was a hundred years old. This had been one of those times.

After what had seemed like an hour, John had begun talking. He said that before and during the Kennedy time, in the 1960s, the CIA wasn't as controlled as it was now. The agents generally made their decisions based on the knowledge they had and rarely waited for approval for their actions. He claimed it was basically its own entity and answered to no one. Then he backtracked in time to a few years before that and told her how John Kennedy's father had raised his sons for the presidency. The Kennedy boys had been born to be presidents, and their father intended to make them a great political dynasty. According to John, JFK's father made some deals with some very powerful people—some in the CIA and some members of the Mafia.

These two groups, supposedly, could control enough of the American vote to guarantee the outcome of a presidential election, of course, for a price. The story was, Kennedy's father didn't have a problem with the price tag attached and John F. Kennedy would become the president of the United States. Naturally, all went as planned, except that JFK wouldn't follow the rules. He didn't want to "pay the price" his father had agreed to pay.

According to John, threats flew back and forth for a while, with JFK threatening to expose the CIA and the Mafia. Eventually, the Mafia began to throw around threats about killing Kennedy's associates and family members. JFK erroneously assumed the bad guys would decide to not take the risk, and he could run the country as he felt it should be run. Kennedy had formed a close diplomatic relationship with the Korean minister at the time. Morgan couldn't remember the reason, but the powers that be decided that JFK and the Korean guy both needed to be eliminated.

Trying to send Kennedy a message, the CIA had sent three young American operatives to Korea to eliminate Kennedy's stronghold there and to try to warn the doomed president of the United States. Somehow the three young men did manage to get close enough to the Korean to kill him. John knew the man who had pulled the trigger on the rifle. Shortly thereafter, the three men, dressed as American tourists, walked through the Korean airport and boarded a plane back to the States. Kennedy either did not understand the message being sent or chose to ignore it because three weeks later, Kennedy would be assassinated as well.

John F. Kennedy was, of course, told of his friend's death. Kennedy was also told that if he rode in the parade, he would, most assuredly, be assassinated that fateful day in Dallas, Texas. Kennedy, for whatever reason, felt sure he would be safe; no one would possibly even seriously consider trying to kill him in front of thousands of people. John F. Kennedy was fatally shot, sitting by his wife, Jackie Kennedy, while riding in the convertible in the parade. Both shots came from behind Kennedy. One round seemed to be shot from the grassy knoll, and the other directly behind the president. Neither shot originated from the area Oswald was said to be. Lee Harvey Oswald was only around to observe the parade, like thousands of others, but the CIA immediately seized him and turned him over to the Secret Service, complete with immediate, irrefutable evidence. Oswald, of course, was murdered shortly thereafter by a distraught American trying to avenge his president's death. Oswald could not have ever gone to trial as the evidence might not have held up. John's story concluded with a comment about a multifaceted covert operation that had taken months to plan and less than forty-eight hours to complete and would take years to cover up.

Morgan turned the shower off and stepped back into reality. Here she was, in an FBI agent's home, all kinds of law enforcement agencies were looking for her, and there was actually a warrant for her arrest for murder. She didn't have a home anymore, and she couldn't even go see her kids. It sure seemed like a hell of a mess to her. Personally, though, she had taken John's Kennedy story as a ridiculous tale meant to impress her in some weird way, and she was going to feel like an idiot repeating it to Frank. She honestly thought he'd throw her out of his house by the time she got to that part of the tale. She was very, very wrong.

CHAPTER 6

"You're a very popular young woman tonight," said Frank as she emerged into the living room. "Your picture has been all over the television. Doesn't look much like you, though. I doubt if anyone who saw us today would recognize you." He was smiling again, which, for some strange reason, made her furious. Morgan guessed it was because he didn't find much too funny about the state of her affairs.

Frank handed her a cup of coffee, and she lit a cigarette and jumped into her Kennedy tale. Morgan figured the sooner she got that over with, the sooner she could move on to something else. Frank stopped her only once to ask a question and to grab a pen and paper to take notes. Then he had her repeat the story three more times.

"What's the big deal about this, Frank?" she asked, confused.

"Don't you realize you're talking about the death of a United States president?"

"Yeah, I know that, but it happened before I was even born. And it seems very irrelevant to me about what's going on here. I think we're wasting time." Morgan was tired. She was scared. She really did not care what had happened to John F. Kennedy.

"OK, Morgan. Now I don't care if we're skipping the order of things here. Tell me anything, I mean, anything else John said to you." It was two o'clock in the morning, and she was tired. By this time, the coffee wasn't working any longer, and she only wanted to collapse. Morgan noticed, to her amazement, that retelling these stories was very tiring. Mentally, she was confusing herself, her brain exhausted. Of course, she was worried about her daughters too. There was just so much to think about right now. It was overwhelming.

Frank, on the other hand, seemed excited. He'd read his notes and ask questions. He'd tell her to repeat the story again. He'd ask more questions. He didn't seem tired in the least. He was a highly rated interviewer, and he knew that as Morgan became mentally exhausted, she would vary her story if she was not being truthful.

"What else? You've got to tell me everything!" Frank was excited.

Morgan thought he had probably lost his mind—maybe some disillusioned FBI agent who had lost his wife and kids and needed to fill some kind of void in his life. "I don't know anything else, Frank, really. Just that John said once that there were people, I think he referred to them as Black Ops or something like that. He said they were doctors, lawyers, judges, bankers, etc.—all types of professional people, well trained in specific areas, on call for assignments, without explanation for the government. People who could be contacted at a moment's notice to handle a 'situation.' He never told me what kind of situation, and I only asked once. I didn't know the Kennedys, the Oswalds, or the Korean. I'm just repeating stories that don't mean anything to me."

"What other government assassinations did John tell you about?" Morgan could only recall one more, but it was more a combination of what John had told her and what she had done. It was something that had haunted her for more than a year.

One day, John had called her on the phone and asked if she had any kind of address finder on her computer. Morgan told him she did, as do most people with internet access and especially people in business. He asked her to drive over to his house and talk to him. Naturally, she ran right over. John had said he had a friend, an old acquaintance, he had known during the war. This man currently used the name of Ricky Davis as an alias.

Ricky was a truck driver by day and an assassin for the right money. Ricky owned his tractor trailer and had won the National Truck Driver Rodeo competition the last three years in a row. John said this was a big deal. Additionally, John said Ricky's own wife didn't know who he really was and the reason he drove a truck was because he needed a good excuse to get out of the house when he had a contract to fulfill. John said Ricky needed an address on someone he had been hired to kill but didn't want to search on the internet because it could be acquired and traced back to him if investigated by upper-level agencies. John couldn't look for the man because it would connect him to the potential target. John was sure he could trust Morgan, so he asked if she could find an address for him.

Morgan told him she would see what she could do, that she thought he was full of it. And they had gone into his bedroom and made love for the rest of the afternoon. Morgan easily found the address John needed. If this was someone who knew he was being hunted, he was doing a rather poor job of hiding himself. She gave John the address and phone number the next day and assumed she had passed some sort of test of loyalty with him. She didn't believe a word of his story about the hit man or the contract on Randall Gray.

Two days later, John called Morgan again and asked her to meet him in the parking lot of the gas station where they had originally met to smoke cigarettes when she was managing at the day-care center. Always obliging, Morgan hopped in her car and drove down to the station. She pulled up in the parking beside John's truck and asked why they were there. He said he wanted her to meet someone.

John pointed across the parking lot to a tractor trailer rig, and a man waved at Morgan. John said it was Ricky, and now that Ricky knew who she was, it was imperative that she did not tell anyone she had looked up the address. Morgan didn't say anything and drove home. The skating rink had been allowed to reopen by this time, but Morgan didn't go to work. She had a couple of part-time employees fill in for her, and of course, John was ever present to supervise. She didn't call him. She couldn't think of anything to say. Morgan still didn't quite believe the Ricky story, but if it wasn't true, she felt it was a horrible practical joke. If it were true, then she had just seriously become an accessory to a murder of a man she did not even know. Nope, couldn't find anything funny about it.

The following week, she got a phone call early in the morning. The City of Clarkston Police were calling to let her know the rink had been burglarized and she needed to secure the building. All the windows and front glass doors were broken, and anything inside of value was gone— the sound system, compact discs, lighting equipment, etc. There were no suspects, but the police would put a detective on the case and see what they could do. Oddly enough, John wasn't around that morning.

The skating rink was closed for another ten days as Morgan filed the insurance forms, cleaned up the mess, and ordered new equipment. Try as they might, the police just couldn't get any leads and had no suspects in the case. Morgan talked to John once during this time, but it was a conversation that was strictly business. Otherwise, they didn't speak or see each other.

Around this time, Morgan was starting to get stressed. Between the mess with John and the constant problems with the skating rink, she was getting a bit edgy. She was having trouble sleeping. She found herself lying on her sofa, watching television at three in the morning. Right at the moment when the movie ended and the television station switched to a commercial and there was a second of silence, Morgan heard a noise.

The sound was obviously outside, but it was still close to her house. It had been a strange noise, and she couldn't think of what the sound was. Morgan looked out of her windows and couldn't see anything. She walked around to her patio door and looked out over the back porch. Standing there on the porch—the same porch where she and John had sat so many mornings, drinking coffee—was Ricky the hit man.

Morgan was too scared to speak or move, so she just stood there like an idiot. Ricky was standing there, staring at her, but in front of him was another man. The man's mouth was taped, and when she saw that, she understood what the noise had been. It had been the man's muffled cries for help. Morgan's eyes locked on the man's eyes, and she knew he saw her looking through the door. He struggled, couldn't get free, and tried to scream again. His hands were tied behind his back, and Ricky's arm was wrapped around the man's neck.

All this happened in a matter of seconds, she was sure, but even as Morgan remembered the scene, it was as if it played out in slow-motion. Ricky had smiled at her and raised his right arm up into the air. He pointed a gun at Morgan through the door, and she still couldn't move. Then he bent his arm, placed the gun against the side of the man's head, and pulled the trigger. The man was staring at her as he died. Ricky then carried the dead man and left the porch. As they were leaving, Morgan saw, from the shadows in her yard, that another man was walking away. She couldn't tell for sure who he was, but his silhouette closely resembled that of John Henson.

CHAPTER 7

Naturally, Morgan panicked. She couldn't be sure but was fairly certain that had they meant to harm her, they would have done it then. Morgan took what had happened to be a message to her. About what? It wasn't really clear. But she had gotten the message and just wanted to get the hell out. By dawn, she had enough clothes packed for her daughters and her for two weeks. Morgan woke her children and ran to the car and drove straight to Atlanta before ever stopping to change them from their nightgowns or to feed them breakfast.

Morgan checked in to a hotel near the Atlanta airport. She figured if they needed to leave town quickly, they could hop on a plane to somewhere. She just didn't know to where. By this time, her checking and savings accounts had diminished considerably, and she was beginning to get seriously worried about money. She couldn't ever keep the skating rink open long enough to make enough money to pay the employees and make a profit. By this time, Morgan was getting behind on her mortgage and every bill imaginable. She knew if she couldn't turn the financial situation around very quickly, bankruptcy was going to be her only option. Morgan did, however, still have enough money to get the three of them on a plane and enough to hide out in hotels for a couple of weeks if necessary. There was small comfort there.

Sometime after lunch, just as she had laid her daughters down for a nap, the hotel phone rang. Morgan answered, thinking it would be the front desk as she hadn't told anyone where they were going. Naturally, she was wrong again. It was Lucas Brown. "Hello, Morgan. How's it going?" he asked.

Morgan's mind was spinning. She had no idea why Lucas was calling or how he knew where she was. Morgan did know it meant that for some reason, someone had been watching them. Trying to hide at the hotel had been nothing but a waste of time. Morgan quickly decided to try to act like she was calm. Surely, the idea had been to scare and confuse her, which they had accomplished, but she was hoping to throw some small kink in their plans by trying not to act rattled. "Hey, Lucas," she answered. "We're doing great, and you?"

"Never better. Listen, I hear John's looking for you. Thought you might want to know."

"I'll see him at the rink, but thanks."

"Sure thing. Hey, did you see this afternoon's paper? The Clarkston Police found a decapitated body not too far from your house early this morning. The body was just lying on the side of the road. Strange world, huh?"

"Yeah, Lucas. It's a strange world all right. Look, I've got to go, got a meeting to make."

"Have a safe trip."

"I intend to," Morgan said and hung up the phone. Morgan took great pride knowing she had managed not to ask him why he was really calling, why he knew where she was, or why he was so interested in a decapitated body. John had told her a long time before that sometimes the best thing you could do was to do nothing. He had also said that it was crucial that your enemy never saw you react to anything. Morgan thought she had done well on the phone but then realized Lucas knew what had happened, knew she was hiding, and knew damned well she was scared out of her mind. Who did Morgan think she was kidding? She felt so incredibly stupid.

Morgan managed, though, to wait several hours before going down to the lobby to get the evening edition of the *Atlanta Journal*. The story was below the fold but on the front page nonetheless. According to the article, the man's then unidentified body had been found tossed on the side of Highway 27, the road leading to her home. Although his head, which was still missing, had been chopped off, the deceased had been identified through fingerprints. His name was Randall Gray—the man whose address Morgan had found for John and Ricky.

If anyone was watching, then they would have seen her race to the ladies' room in the hotel lobby where she became violently ill. Eventually, Morgan managed to wash her face off in the restroom and ride the elevator back upstairs to their room. Morgan's daughters wanted to go swimming, but she insisted on room service for dinner and a night of watching television. They grumbled about it but managed to find a kid's movie that caught their attention. Morgan stared out the window all night.

The sun was coming up by the time she had finished telling Frank about Ricky, the contract killer, and Randall Gray, the man Morgan helped along to his death. Telling the story had drained her. She wondered a time or two if Frank would simply arrest her for murder and be done with the whole mess. He didn't, though. Once again, Frank had madly scribbled notes but never interrupted the story the first time through.

"I know you're not going to ask me to tell you that again," Morgan said. "I really can't. I feel sick when I think about it, never mind talking about the damn thing."

Frank looked up from his notes, started to say something, and apparently thought better of it. Instead, he stood up, stretched, and walked over to the window. Looking outside, he could see the snow had stopped during the night, but the roads and yards were still white, which would work to their benefit later. He turned around and stared at Morgan, his eyes softening a little as he did. "Ms. Morgan, you are either insane, a marvelous liar, or in a hell of a lot of trouble. Honestly, I wouldn't believe you, except you were with me when they're claiming John was murdered. So assuming you're in more trouble than probably either one of us can handle, we've got to figure this out quickly. You sit here and rest, and I'm going back to the bedroom and make a couple of phone calls."

Frank quickly decided, after a few phone calls, that he had to act immediately but was afraid Morgan was rapidly reaching her breaking point.

He decided to ask her about herself and not her current situation. "Tell me about yourself, Morgan," said Frank.

"You know everything I know," she said. She was still obviously agitated.

"C'mon, Morgan. Tell me about before now, when things were good for you."

Morgan sat quietly for a moment and then relented. "OK," she said and began another story for Frank. "I grew up on a little farm. We had a great family—Mom and Dad home every night, few fights, family dinner at the kitchen table every night, church every Sunday. They thought I could do no wrong. They'd be very disappointed now, by the way."

"Keep going," urged Frank.

"I did great in high school and started college, and then my parents died in a car crash. Everything kind of sucked after that. I immediately went from having security and safety to having nothing but adult issues and no guidance. Hell, I was only nineteen years old then. I had been really sheltered, even though I didn't know it, and I didn't know anything about the real world.

"I dropped out of college because I just wasn't sure what I wanted to do. So I got my EMT certification and went to work in Atlanta. I thought maybe I could help some people. I liked it for a while. But the more I saw—and I saw a lot—I thought it just started making me sad. Sure, we saved our share of folks who had car wrecks or heart attacks or strokes, but so many of them were young ladies, usually not much older than I was.

"There were young women who had started out with dreams but, somehow or the other, got mixed up with the wrong guy. And he either got her on drugs or into prostitution. Sometimes both. When the girl would try to leave him, inevitably, he would beat the hell out of her. Sometimes the guy would beat her too much, and we'd get the call to go help. Usually, we could keep them alive, but they almost always went back to what they were doing. They'd always say they had no other choice or didn't know anything different. They were already beaten down for life by some man who couldn't care less about them. After a time, that got kind of depressing to me, so I decided to move on.

"I went back to college," continued Morgan. "And I met my daughters' father. We fell in love, got married, and had my two daughters in three years. I thought we were forever, but he decided it was more fun to lay around all day and never work and let me support us. That wouldn't have been so bad, but he wouldn't help with the kids either. So eventually, I gave up, asked for a divorce, and he went away as soon as I stopped paying his bills. I guess I was only good for the paycheck."

"That's a shame, Morgan," said Frank. "I don't know why he didn't appreciate you more."

Morgan shrugged. There wasn't really any anger, just sadness at the loss of a life with her husband she had thought would work out well. "I don't know," she said. "He never explained. He just said he wasn't going to hang around if I didn't support him. I said I wasn't going to keep doing that, and he left. I had a little bit of money left from my parents' life insurance, so I bought the skating rink and day care and figured I could provide for my daughters."

"And then you met John?" Frank asked.

"Yep, and look at me now. How in the hell I have put myself and my daughters in this mess is beyond me. All I want to do is give them a good life. Simple. It's not supposed to be this hard."

"We're going to figure this out, Morgan," said Frank. "Somehow. What are you planning on doing next?"

"I don't know." Morgan shrugged. "Hopefully something I can do with my daughters. Maybe an animal rescue. Of course, I have to stay alive to be able to do anything."

Frank had listened intently to Morgan. He didn't hear a druggie or a prostitute or a vengeful woman hell-bent on revenge. He didn't hear a psychotic person although he was sure Morgan would have a mental breakdown soon if some of her pressure wasn't relieved. All Frank heard was a young woman who had made terrible choices with men and who only wanted to be loved and to love her children. Frank then knew what he felt he had to do.

Frank stood up and said, "Morgan, come with me. I've got to show you something."

Morgan stood up and followed Frank. They went downstairs to his basement. Once in the basement, Frank walked to the far back of the room and unlocked a door. "Come here, please," he said.

"Why?" Morgan asked. She wasn't particularly thrilled about walking through a door in a basement.

"Morgan, come here. You have got to trust me. This is my gun room. There's a sofa and a television and a little mini fridge with some water and sodas in there. You can sit in here and watch TV or take a nap. You'll be safe in here."

"Where are you going to be? I don't want to be here alone."

"I've got to do some things, and you cannot go with me."

"No, Frank. I don't want to do this. I'll just leave, and you can find me later."

"Morgan, where do you think you'll go? Look, there's a pistol here on the counter. Do you know how to fire a handgun?"

Morgan nodded and added, "Yes, I grew up on a farm, remember? Another thing my daddy taught me was how to shoot when I was eight or nine years old. I could shoot better than most boys in our town."

"OK, great," Frank continued. "Listen now. When I leave, lock this door. Do not, do not open it for anyone but me, no matter what anyone may say. When I come back, I will say "Fallen angel," and you will know it's me, OK? Morgan, you have somewhat convinced me you are really a good woman, an angel—I'm not sure yet—but definitely fallen," Frank said with a smile.

Morgan didn't think this was OK at all. She didn't want to be locked in a room, and she damn sure didn't want to be left alone. She was thinking she would leave and just run as soon as Frank left. No, she didn't like this plan, and she wasn't going to play. She was ready to leave. But maybe, just maybe, God had put Frank in her life at definitely the lowest point. She didn't have any other good options.

"All right," Morgan said, silently praying Frank was indeed a good man and not simply leaving her to retrieve those who wanted her dead.

"Good girl. Oh, and don't leave while I'm gone. I'm serious, Morgan. They will kill you. You have got to stay put. Promise? OK, now raise your right hand and swear, Morgan, that you will not leave." Frank smiled while saying this, and she realized he was trying to make her laugh and maybe to offer a little glimmer of hope.

"I guess." She sighed, and while smiling, she raised her left hand. Frank and Morgan both laughed a little, and for a moment, Morgan hoped they could be friends.

Frank smiled at her and pulled the door shut. Morgan turned on the TV and sat cross-legged on the sofa, pistol in hand. Frank wasn't even out of the house yet, and she was terrified.

He had an idea who might be behind all this, and it scared him—partly because it could be someone who was damn near impossible to stop and partly because Frank was afraid a dark side of him would emerge, consuming his soul. He wasn't sure what he was going to do if he found out what he needed to know, but he knew the only way he could protect Morgan was to find out. He locked Morgan in the gun room in his basement and drove away in the darkness in a pickup truck he kept parked behind his house.

The snow had stopped falling a few hours before, but the roads were still slow. This gave Frank more time to think. He wondered if he had lost his mind. There wasn't much logic in his "need" to protect Morgan. Despite his extensive law enforcement training, he didn't feel any need to be a hero and could easily ride out his remaining years until retirement. No, there was more to it than just that. He was almost certain Morgan would die without his help and her children would live without a good mother. It was not really his problem, but it bothered him anyway. Frank had to be sure, had to know that it was indeed the people he feared who wanted to kill Morgan, and he had to know if their plan was already in action.

He couldn't obtain the necessary information through legal means as that would take far too long. He couldn't ask his law enforcement friends for help either as that would jeopardize their jobs and retirement just as he was risking his own. If he was correct about who these people were, they would have little trouble killing him and much less trouble killing Morgan. He knew he had to find the answers to his questions, and he had very little time to find them. He also knew he was going to have to use some methods that would not be legal without a court order. Morgan would be dead long before any of that could be arranged.

Frank drove to the Peachtree DeKalb Airport and rented a helicopter. He selected an R44 Raven II because it was relatively fast, and he could easily sell the idea he was just renting it for a "practice" flight. Everyone knew him there; most were his friends. He had learned to fly here. The Atlanta news helicopters flew from this airport, and Frank had flown with them all. Sure, a few questioned why he wasn't flying his FBI chopper, which was much cooler, and several questioned why he would be going up so late on a snowy night. But Frank already had established his answer—taking a break, too many cases, and he needed to clear his mind. He had much professional flight time, and the current weather conditions were very challenging for practice. He hoped they would buy his story even though he knew they would all feel it was too risky. They all knew him and liked him, so no one questioned too deeply. Frank knew they wouldn't—at least not directly to him. But after he left, they would talk and wonder if Frank was actually that good or if he had lost his mind.

Frank performed his preflight routine at the airport. He realized he would have two hours of fuel—plenty of time if he didn't see anything but not nearly enough if something happened. He filed an instrument flight plan with air traffic controllers, which he was required to do, and they questioned the safety of his flying in the current weather conditions as well.

"Nothing will happen," Frank said aloud to himself, and he ascended into the night.

The first order of business was that Frank had to stay under the airspace of the Hartsfield-Jackson Atlanta International Airport so he could observe what he needed to see. He called air traffic control on the radio to request permission to do what few pilots knew they could do—cross Hartsfield airport at five hundred feet exactly and fly precisely midfield across all four runways while jets are landing under them. No one in their right mind would have requested this in the current weather. Frank was grateful he knew this because, otherwise, he would never have enough fuel to carry out his plan. Permission was granted but not without a few choice comments from the FAA controllers asking Frank if he thought he was Chuck Yeager, the most famous test pilot in history, because no one else would willingly fly in such conditions. And then Frank flew into the night.

A few minutes later, Frank was hovering on the south side of Stone Mountain. Somewhat out of sight from his target, Frank found he was enjoying the flight. He enjoyed the freedom of flight and had reassured himself he was overreacting, being paranoid. He spotted the area he was looking for—a bar where "normal" people didn't go, and if they did, they were lucky to leave alive. They damn sure didn't return if they were lucky enough to be allowed to leave.

Frank watched for a few minutes. He convinced himself this would be a good practice flight, and he could reassure himself he was overreacting. Yes, Morgan was in a lot of trouble. Yes, she was suffering some really serious consequences for having a relationship with the wrong man. Yes, she was charged with a crime she didn't commit, but that didn't necessarily mean she was going to be murdered. Frank was about to return to the airport, and then he saw what he dreaded the most.

Looking through his Zeiss binoculars, compliments of the FBI, Frank watched as the man who was orchestrating Morgan's problems came out of the bar. Checking his car for any GPS trackers, the man thought he had determined no one was following him. Thankfully, he never considered a helicopter would be hovering slightly behind Stone Mountain and watching him. Frank's calmness disappeared quickly as he realized where the car was headed—directly toward his home. How in the hell they knew to head in the directions of his house eluded him. He had taken extraordinary measures, or lack thereof, to ensure no one would connect him to Morgan. There was no way he could imagine that anyone could associate him with Morgan. But they had, and they were on their way. Checking his gauges, Frank realized he had approximately forty-five minutes of fuel left, probably not enough, but he knew he had to tail his suspect. Morgan may very well die tonight if he lost the car. Frank was also acutely aware he, too, could die if the weather worsened. None of that mattered, though, because he had to know.

Frank needed to call Morgan and be sure she understood to stay in the gun room. It's difficult to make phone calls while flying a helicopter because the pilot is always using both hands and both feet. Phone calls had to be quick. Morgan answered on the third ring.

"Morgan, listen," said Frank. "I don't have long to talk, but you stay in the gun room with the door locked. And do not open it for anyone! Especially if they say I sent them for you! I will come to the door, and I will say "Fallen angel." And then you can open the door. Do not open that door for any other reason! Do you understand?"

Morgan's mind was racing, and she really couldn't comprehend what he was telling her. She could hear the sound of a helicopter and wondered what the hell Frank was doing.

"Damn it, Morgan! Do you hear me? This isn't a joke! Don't leave that room under any circumstance!"

"OK" was all Morgan could say. She knew there was no point in asking a totally ridiculous question about what he was doing.

Once he was off the phone, Frank was free to concentrate on what he needed to be doing. Once the car was within ten miles of his home, Frank called the Hartsfield tower to request a midfield pass over at five hundred feet coming in from three miles north, heading south. And for the first time ever in his flying career doing this, in these conditions, the tower advised Frank to stand by in current position because military helicopters were departing the airport. Frank's mind almost exploded. This simply could not be happening, not now. He knew he would lose the suspect and might not be able to find the car again. Maybe they would get to Morgan before Frank could, and God only knew what would happen then. Frank was more frustrated than he had ever been in his life.

Suddenly, by the grace of God, the radio crackled, and Frank was given clearance to proceed. Sweating profusely, even though it was incredibly cold, Frank pushed the helicopter to its maximum speed of 150 knots. Everything he was doing this night was out of character for him, but he was consumed with a sense of urgency, a gut-wrenching need to catch up with the car speeding in the direction of his home. Once he spotted the vehicle on Interstate 75, only five miles from his home, Frank relaxed a bit and was once again able to focus on his suspect.

Frank had left his FBI vehicle parked in the driveway, hoping anyone nearby would assume he might be home. Perhaps the suspect did because the car drove past Frank's driveway slowly and parked in the driveway of a neighbor's house. The neighbor, Frank knew, was out of town, on vacation. Apparently, the suspect knew this too because he backed into the driveway so he could have an unobstructed view of Frank's house.

Fifteen minutes passed as Frank watched from above as the suspect surveyed Frank's house. Frank realized this was most likely a planning mission for the man—scope out the territory and return to the bar to construct a plan. The car pulled out of the driveway quietly and drove away into the night with no one in the neighborhood becoming suspicious.

"Damn, he's good," Frank said aloud to no one in particular. He followed the car long enough to ascertain the vehicle was not going to return to his home, and then he had the immediate issue of needing to return to the airport before running out of fuel. It was going to be a close call.

Frank did make it back to the Peachtree DeKalb Airport with four minutes of fuel remaining. He was acutely aware of the damage this would do to his reputation as a supersafe pilot and was equally sure questions would be asked eventually.

Right now, though, Frank asked the ground crew to refuel and gave them an extra hundred bucks for their troubles and said he would appreciate it greatly if they didn't mention this evening's events to anyone. The guys saluted and said, "Yes, sir!" This caused Frank to laugh. He needed to laugh, and he was aware it could possibly be the last time he ever would. Frank had decided on his next move, but with little time to plan, he realized he was probably ending his career and possibly his life. He couldn't think of any other thing he could do.

Frank got back into his vehicle and headed to the bar where the man who had surveilled his home had originally exited. Frank assumed the man would be returning to the bar to share the information he had gathered. Frank hoped so at least. He realized these were some very dangerous people, people Morgan had no chance to beat in any circumstance. Frank was Morgan's only hope, and he knew this. Frank had once believed miracles could happen, but years in his profession had caused him to lose faith. He also knew he was going to need a miracle to keep Morgan and himself alive.

As he maneuvered the slick roads as quickly as possible, his mind began to wander. He couldn't quite understand why Morgan was becoming so important to him. Was it because she had no other option? Was it because he had become such a lost soul he simply no longer cared? Why would he be willing to risk his career and his retirement on some young woman that he had only just met? Why did he care? Maybe it was simply because it was the right thing to do and the only thing to do.

The roads were deserted. Covered with a thin layer of ice, no one in his right mind would be out driving. There was nothing to see, except his windshield wipers removing the mist gathering on his windshield and the beams of the headlights reflecting from the pavement. Frank thought of his wife and children.

He had been very proud of his family—was still damn proud of his children but so very disappointed on how his life had turned out with his wife. The children had all grown into marvelous adults. Three daughters, all young adults, had promising careers in front of them. The son, a member of the coast guard, was a national hero who had received commendations for a heroic rescue the boy had carried out on his own. Frank was beyond amazed at his son's heroism, but his son had told him he had just done what Frank had taught him to do as a child and it was no big deal. Frank was proud of his son's humility and the path he had chosen to follow. He was equally as proud of his daughters. One was a nurse for a air-evac service which provided critical care for extremely ill or injured patients while transporting them to a hospital. Another daughter was in the music industry and doing quite well, and the other daughter was a computer specialist who frequently worked with some of the largest businesses in the country. Frank loved his family dearly, and each of them had a very special place in his heart.

Maybe his wife had gotten tired of the long hours Frank worked, or maybe she had grown weary of wondering if he would come home each night or end up in the hospital or, worse, dead. Maybe she had never really loved him, but Frank thought she had at one time. Maybe she simply grew weary of trying to reach out to him after his father had died. Frank had been exceptionally close to his father, and part of his heart had broken when his father died and he wasn't there to help him. There was so much Frank felt he had done wrong and so many regrets. He had tried so damn hard his entire life to simply serve his country, but in doing so, he had failed in not spending more time with his family. Frank sighed deeply and tried to concentrate on his plan to save Morgan. Somehow, Frank was beginning to feel his questionably illegal act could somehow be his one chance left for redemption.

Frank knew what he was planning on doing was wrong. He was about to throw away a twenty-four-year career in law enforcement—a spotless career marked only with commendations and awards. Never had Frank killed anyone when he had any other option. Never had Frank arrested someone he felt was innocent nor had he taken any bribes. Now Frank was about to willingly break the law to possibly save his "fallen angel" and possibly was going to go to prison. If he wasn't arrested, it most likely was going to be because he was dead. There was no time for him to go through legal channels to try to help Morgan as some of the very people trying to kill her were part of the government, people who were violating the American system as it was meant to be. There were no other options he could find. Frank was giving up the last part of his life of which he believed he had achieved some success.

Somehow, Frank was beginning to feel this illegal act could somehow be his one chance left for redemption—his final chance to somehow save his soul.

"God help me," Frank whispered to himself. Once, Frank had believed God was in the "success business" to help us succeed if one had the faith to try to not give up on Him. Frank sure hoped this was true.

Frank arrived at his destination—an abandoned building just down the street from the bar. Frank knew he was about to cross the line, reaching a point where he couldn't return to his safety net. He would no longer have the option of turning Morgan in to authorities. Hell, he probably would no longer have the option of being a law enforcement authority. He also knew there was no other choice unless he was just going to willingly let Morgan be murdered. He knew his soul would be lost forever if he decided to go that route.

Frank was also acutely aware that he couldn't just kill the leader of this group because the remaining members would simply double their efforts to find him. Frank's only hope was to somehow instill some fear in them—hopefully enough fear to buy him a few extra hours. Frank was not completely sure these men were even capable of experiencing fear, but he was going to do his best to find out.

Many years prior, Frank had been trained as a sniper by a gentleman named Carlos Hathcock, frequently referred to as White Feather at the Georgia Public Safety Training Center. Carlos had used a Winchester Model 70, commonly known to hunters as a .30-06 with a Unertl scope. Frank still used the same weapon but with an upgraded scope and a suppressor, frequently referred to as a silencer. Frank never spoke of his duties as a sniper for the FBI or his training of future snipers. This was just a hidden part of his life he shared with no one. He knew that any man who was proud of killing, even to save others, should never be allowed to serve this country.

Frank had chosen this building for a reason. It was about three-fourths of a mile away from the bar, and the bar was lighted out-front, making a clean shot for Frank easiest. The shot would not be heard from a distance of five hundred yards, and in an area with vehicles passing by, no one would be able to determine where the shots were coming from or from how many shooters. Feeling resigned to his decision, Frank climbed to the roof of the building, set up his rifle, and patiently waited for the men to exit the bar.

As was their custom, the men exited the bar around 3:00 a.m. This night, there were five of them—four motorcycles and a car. Each checked his ride for any sign of a tracking device. As they were getting ready to depart, Frank fired his first shot. Exactly as planned, the bullet hit precisely one foot to the left of the man who had been scoping out Frank's house and went through the driver's side door and passed through the passenger door. The only sound the men heard was the bullet striking the car, and they all immediately looked down at the car door to see the hole in the vehicle. The men were beginning to comprehend this was a gunshot when Frank took aim again.

Frank fired four more shots, each about a foot away from each gang member and each bullet piercing the fuel tank of the men's motorcycle. The gang members scrambled for cover but couldn't decide where to hide. They were certain there were multiple shooters, but who? No one would dare attack them. No one who had any intention of remaining alive. Frank stayed on the building. Looking through his scope long enough to see the leader of these men, the man who had been just yards from Frank's house earlier in the evening mouthed the words "It has to be him. It is Frank." The men ran back into the bar for some cover while they discussed what to do next.

Frank quickly left his shooting site, got back into his truck, and drove back as quickly as he could to Morgan. He needed to get her away, and he knew they wouldn't have too much time to leave.

Morgan stayed in the gun room as Frank had asked, but she was scared. She had every reason to be scared, but the longer Frank was gone, the more her imagination ran wild. Her senses were magnified. She could hear everything—the television they had left on upstairs, the furnace turning on and off, her heartbeat, and every breath she took. Frank had been gone a few hours, but to Morgan, it seemed an eternity. Maybe he was dead. Maybe he was getting the GBI to come arrest her. Maybe she was just wrong about everything. She didn't know. Morgan had never been so unsure about anything in her life. She was panicking, and she knew it but was unable to calm down.

Morgan heard the car tires sliding over the icy sludge covering the street and driveway leading up to Frank's house. She heard the car door open and quietly shut. It was barely audible, but she heard it all. She heard the lock on the garage door turn and the door open and close quietly. Suddenly, she was certain Lucas Brown was coming downstairs to kill her. Frank had been gone too long, and Lucas had most likely won. She knew her only chance was to shoot Lucas immediately as he opened the door to the gun room. She wasn't sure she could pull the trigger, but she was certain she had to if she wanted to live.

Morgan raised the gun and pulled back the hammer. Holding the gun as steady as she could, she pointed the revolver directly at the door. She was amazed at how cold she was, but sweat was dripping from her forehead into her eyes. She couldn't do much other than try to blink the sweat away. She damn sure wasn't lowering the gun. She was shaking so badly it took all her strength to just hold the gun up, and she had no idea if she could pull the trigger.

Footsteps came down the stairs, slowly and quietly. Each step was carefully placed to not slip and not make excessive noise. The faint sound of each step echoed in Morgan's head so loud she felt her head would explode until finally the footsteps approached the door. Morgan knew he was there. She wasn't sure who *he* was, but she knew someone was at the door, waiting to come to her, maybe coming to kill her.

"Fallen angel." She heard him say, but she couldn't tell whose voice it was. She desperately needed it to be Frank, but she just couldn't tell. Morgan couldn't speak.

"Fallen angel," said the voice a little louder. "Morgan, are you awake?"

She still couldn't speak and stood there frozen, pointing the gun. She tried to breathe, and even that was hard.

"Morgan, I'm opening the door. Please answer me!"

Morgan couldn't answer. She wanted to hide but couldn't think of where to go. She was shaking so badly she doubted she could walk anyway. She was surprised she was still standing.

The doorknob turned, and the door slowly opened. "Fallen angel," the voice repeated, and Morgan knew. She saw Lucas there, smiling that damn grin he had.

"Stop, Lucas," she managed to say. "I will kill you."

The silhouette stood still, looking at her. Morgan was certain it was Lucas, smiling at her, laughing as he knew he had beaten her. He would win again because he always did. No one could beat the great Lucas Brown.

"Damn it, Lucas! I will kill you!" she managed to say.

"Honey, it's me, Frank. Put the gun down. You're safe. It's me," said the shadow.

Morgan blinked and tried to see clearly. It was dark in the room by her choice. She wouldn't want Lucas to see her clearly. Now she squinted to try to see the man standing before her. She did not lower her gun.

"Morgan, it's me. It's Frank," said the voice. "I'm turning on the light, OK? Don't shoot me, Morgan. You're the fallen angel, remember? Only you and I talked about that. It's just me, Frank. I will not hurt you."

Frank switched on the light, and Morgan almost pulled the trigger and shot him. She was certain it was Lucas's face she saw, but she heard Frank's voice. She knew she was going insane. As her eyes adjusted to the light, Lucas's face disappeared and Frank's image slowly appeared, washing away her fear.

Morgan slowly lowered the gun. "My god, Frank, I almost shot you" was all she could say.

"I know, honey. It's OK. Give me the gun, please."

Morgan slowly handed him the gun and sat down on the sofa. Never had she been so relieved to see anyone in her life. Never had she realized she could actually kill someone even though she didn't want to do so. Morgan realized she wasn't sure what she was possibly capable of doing if scared enough. Frank realized this as well. Frank slowly took the gun from Morgan's hand and sat beside her on the sofa. Neither one spoke for several minutes.

Morgan flicked on the television and lay down on the sofa. The early morning news show was just beginning, and John's murder, along with the statewide search for her, was the opening story. She watched wide-eyed as pictures of both John and her were shown on the television screen. Anyone with any information about her whereabouts was to contact the authorities immediately. There was even a reward for information leading to Morgan's arrest. The story continued, but she fell asleep. The dream began as it had dozens of times before.

Morgan is in a deserted hallway, just standing there, trying to figure out which way to walk. She hears a noise coming from the far end of the hall and turns to see what it is. Briefly, she can't see anything. But after a moment, she sees a shadow emerging. Morgan walks toward the shadow, wanting to ask whomever it is and how to get out of the hall. As she begins to speak, the figure steps into the light, and she can see Randall Gray. His eyes are staring at her the same way they were the night he was murdered on her porch. He never says anything but just keeps walking. Morgan starts crying and asks him to please forgive her. She tries to tell him she didn't know what was happening, that she hadn't believed John, and she certainly wouldn't have ever given Ricky or John his address if she had. Randall just shakes his head. Finally, he stops walking. He shakes his head slowly and says, "You have no idea what you have done." Then Morgan screams.

Morgan woke up with a jump. Her hands were shaking, and her forehead was covered with perspiration. She sat up and tried to calm down. Looking at the clock, she found she had only been asleep thirty-eight minutes, nothing like a good night's rest.

CHAPTER 8

Lucas had been awake for hours. He was nervous and excited. He loved a good chase and knew it would be over by the end of the day, but he was still worried about what John had said. *How much was everything? Damn old fool was only supposed to watch her at the day-care center and run her out of the skating rink. Really,* Lucas mused, *I should have killed John before he ever resigned as the Williamstown chief of police.* Lucas had made a mistake then; he shouldn't have ever allowed that to happen. But he had softened for his old friend and had allowed it with John's promise that he had everything under control. *Yeah, John certainly had everything under control all right.* Lucas knew he was going to have to explain a lot about this; it was going to be a pain in the ass. But he was confident he could straighten everything out. He was, after all, Lucas Brown.

Lucas's cell phone rang. The voice on the other end informed him that Morgan had not been sighted. They had received a couple of tips from the morning news, but nothing had panned out yet. "She had better be found by lunchtime! We've got to control this!" Lucas yelled into the phone.

"Sir, she's probably snowed in somewhere, and she probably can't get where she's trying to go. We've got taps on half the phones in town and taps on every phone number she's called in the last year. We're really pushing here. Somebody's going to take a fall here if we aren't careful."

"If you don't find her soon, you're going to take a fall. Am I clear?"

"Yes, sir." And the phone went dead.

Lucas was one of the few individuals in Clarkston who did own snow chains. He had placed them on his Jeep Wrangler before the snow had accumulated a quarter of an inch. Lucas was a firm believer in preparedness. He never felt vulnerable unless some turn of events created a situation he had not anticipated. To that end, Lucas tried to plan for every imaginable scenario. He would drive to Atlanta this morning. He knew it would take at least double the normal commute time with the snow. But he had people he needed to speak with, and he didn't want to talk on the telephone.

Lucas would stop and see Jim first. Jim, a veteran police officer, was a lieutenant on the Metro Atlanta SWAT Team. He was an excellent police officer, but personally, his life was totally screwed. Lucas had seen to that. Lucas had managed to plant cocaine in Jim's car and just happened to be in on the bust to be able to save Jim from prosecution. There had also been an incident with a prostitute. Lucas never had any trouble getting Jim to do what he asked. That was just the way Lucas intended.

Lucas made a couple of phone calls during his two-hour drive into Atlanta. He had discovered where Jim was working and made arrangements to meet him in a city park. Lucas wanted to talk. "Hey, buddy!" said Lucas as he walked up to Jim in the park. "Caught any bad guys today?"

Lucas was smiling, and Jim hated that. Actually, he hated Lucas. Jim had known Lucas for years and had met him through his friendship with Robert, and he had regretted every minute of their meeting. Jim knew Lucas had set him up years before with the drug deal, but in Georgia, Lucas Brown might as well have been God himself. "Hey, Lucas, what's up?"

"Did you see the news last night?"

"Yeah, too bad about John. When's the funeral?"

"Are you looking for her, Jim?"

"Who?"

"You had to know about the warrant for Morgan. Are you looking for her?"

"Nope, not my case."

"Make it your case, Jim. I want her today."

"Lucas, it's not my case. I can't go snooping around looking for some lady when I've got a manhunt going on for an escapee. Maybe after I catch this guy."

Lucas reached over and grabbed Jim's coat by the collar. As he did, he pulled his revolver from his holster and pointed the gun under Jim's chin. "Now you listen, fool. I said I want her today, and I expect you'll find her. I don't have time to listen to your whining. Are we clear?"

"What'd she do to you, Lucas? Was she one of your little tramps?"

"Find her today, or you know what'll happen. I don't imagine you'd like being locked up with all the guys you had thrown in the state pen. I hear cops don't do too well there."

"Go to hell, Brown."

"You'll find her, my friend. I know you will." And then Lucas walked away, laughing.

Lucas's second stop was the Georgia Bureau of Investigation office. Naturally, Lucas had lots of friends in this law enforcement office. Most of these guys had worked with him at some time during the past few years. All of them had heard of Lucas's reputation. Daniel Jacobs was sitting at his desk. He knew Lucas would be in this morning, and he knew why. Daniel didn't know, though, what he was going to tell Lucas. They couldn't find her. The city was snowed in, and Lucas had half the damned state looking for some bitch he had a hard-on for. A good many people were getting pissed off, but that wasn't the kind of thing Lucas liked to hear.

Jacobs was sitting alone in the office, so Lucas took off his coat and had a seat across from his friend. "Any news?" asked Lucas.

"Not a word, just like I told you this morning. She's got to be snowed in, Lucas. It's probably going to take a couple of days, at least until the snow thaws."

"That's not good enough. Listen, she might know some things, maybe way more than she should. And the longer she's out, the more chance there is she'll talk to someone. It's not an acceptable risk."

"Lucas, even if she talks, nobody is going to believe what she says. Just calm down."

"Don't tell me to calm down. Don't you realize what's happened? There's no telling what John told her. We might all be dead in a few days if we don't find her!"

Daniel swallowed; his friend was worrying him. Lucas was losing control, and that could only mean trouble for everyone. "Listen, man," said Daniel, "we've got phone taps all over. We've got people at the airports and bus and train stations. We've got her house and businesses staked out. We've got surveillance at every one of her relatives' and friends' homes. There's nowhere else to look right now. She'll show up. She's nothing but a small-town businesswoman and a mother. She can't be a problem. Calm down."

"Dan, my man, if you tell me to calm down again, I'll kill you right now. We're missing something. There's someone she knows you haven't found out about. Find her today." Lucas got up and walked to the door. "I'm sure you'll contact me the second you know where she is, right?"

"You know I will, Lucas."

CHAPTER 9

Morgan was still sitting on the sofa when Frank came back into his living room. "OK, Morgan. I've made some phone calls, and now we've just got to wait. But I need to know a couple more things. Now you said you saw Randall Gray shot on your porch, right?"

Morgan nodded, still remembering the dream.

"You saw someone killed in cold blood right in front of you, but you didn't tell anyone?"

Morgan smiled at that. She vividly remembered the morning in the hotel with her daughters, trying to figure out whom to tell. The city of Williamstown had obviously been out of the question, as well as the Clarke County Police Department and the City of Clarkston Police. Morgan had not felt very secure with those options, given John's reputation and pull in the county. "I did tell someone. I called the GBI from the hotel. I told the lady that answered the phone I knew something about the murder in Clarkston, and she put me on hold for a minute. Then a GBI agent got on the phone and asked me what I knew. I described Ricky as a truck driver I had seen in town and said I had seen Ricky throw the body out of his truck."

"You lied when you reported it?"

"Well, yeah. I was trying to stay relatively uninvolved. Anyway, I told the guy, and he made a big deal about me coming down to his office and talking to him. I told him I couldn't do that, and he said it was illegal to falsely report a crime, punishable by fines and sentences and all that crap. I hung up the phone and checked out of the hotel."

"Do you remember who you talked to when you reported it?"

"Yeah, some guy named Dan Jacobs. He was a real idiot. I didn't like him."

Frank went back to his bedroom again to make more phone calls, and Morgan went in the kitchen to find coffee. She could go a very long time without food, but she couldn't make it very long without cigarettes or coffee. As she was finishing making a pot of coffee, Frank walked in to the kitchen. "I'm going to lie down for about an hour. If you need anything, just help yourself. I'm assuming you're not going to run out the door, right? Remember, you're supposed to be in custody and—"

Morgan cut him off. "I know, I know, I know. I'm not going anywhere."

He smiled at her and retreated down the hall.

Morgan went back to the sofa and thought about John. She still didn't know how she felt about his death. Undoubtedly and probably inexcusably, he had done some terrible things in his lifetime—probably things that weren't going to be forgiven now that he was going to have to explain to a much higher authority. Morgan didn't imagine God much cared who one knew on earth once one had died. She was glad she wasn't there. She was worried enough about what she would have to answer for herself, but at least, her sins didn't include a long list of murders. Maybe there was some small consolation there.

Morgan supposed it was easy to justify anything when it benefited your own cause. She was still saddened though, because the John she had known, particularly in the beginning, had been a very compassionate, loving man. He had listened to her speak of her daughters, dreams, and ambitions. They had made love for hours at a time. They had picnics, fished together, and took long drives. They walked through the woods and always held hands. They had shared some very emotional moments and some very sentimental ones. They had, at times, a particularly close relationship. At least in Morgan's realm of experience, it seemed so. Even after the affair had ended, and she had wanted it too, she had still missed the closeness. Morgan figured she always would.

A few days after the porch episode, Morgan had received another phone call from the City of Clarkston Police. Once again, the skating rink had been vandalized, and once again, unfortunately, there were not any suspects. She never went back to the rink after that phone call. Morgan was too tired mentally to deal with the situation, and she simply could not afford to pay any employees any longer. Morgan spent the afternoon calling employees and informing them how sorry she was but that she would not reopen again. She called everyone but John.

The next afternoon, with a sitter to watch her daughters, Morgan drove all through Williamstown, looking for John. She drove past his home, past the woods where he hunted, and by the lake where they had fished together. She couldn't find him anywhere, so she turned back and was going to wait at his house when she saw his truck pulling out from a little dirt road about a quarter of a mile from his driveway. He waved his arm out of his window and motioned for Morgan to follow.

John turned his truck around, and the two vehicles drove back down the dirt road. The land was posted as being the property of some lumber company. Large areas had been cut, bared of all timber, but the uncut areas were beautiful. Morgan hadn't known this piece of land existed in Williamstown. John turned into a clearing and got out of his truck. He pulled a blanket from the back of his truck and told Morgan to follow. She did, of course.

They had walked through the trees until they had come to another cleared area. A small stream ran across the side of the clearing, and this was where he laid the blanket. The two sat down, and Morgan began telling him about the skating rink and how she just couldn't pay anyone and how she really wasn't sure what she was going to do financially. Morgan told him she was sorry that she couldn't pay him any longer. Morgan knew she sounded pathetic. She didn't really care though. She felt that way.

John never said a word. Instead, he had leaned over, took her face in his hands, and started kissing her. Morgan didn't really want to be kissed, certainly didn't feel like making love as she was doubting all her recent decisions. She said no. Perhaps if she had simply kept her mouth shut then and just let him drive away, things would have turned out differently. That was one thing Morgan didn't guess anyone would ever know.

John got up from the blanket and announced he was going home and that he'd see her later. That made her furious—just the plain nonchalance he exhibited about the situation. Here she was—losing her business, witnessing a murder, talking to a hit man, and being basically harassed by the police—and John was simply going home. Morgan had picked up a clump of dirt and threw it at him. It missed, but he whirled around and glared at her. "You could at least tell me what's going on, you son of a bitch!" she screamed.

John just stood there and stared. Then, suddenly, his face went blank. His eyes were the darkest black she had ever seen, totally without emotion. His forehead was covered with perspiration, and his hands were trembling. He turned and walked to his truck, never uttering a word.

"Tell me what's happening! You owe me that much!"

With that, John threw open the door to his truck and got back out, this time with his pistol. They had stood there, staring at each other, as he raised his arm, aiming the gun at her chest. Morgan knew, if he desired, he could kill her. She knew he was an excellent marksman; he wouldn't miss. She also knew he would get away with killing her. At that moment, she didn't care. Morgan stood there, her blouse still partially unbuttoned, breathing hard enough to hyperventilate. There wasn't any fear, just fury on her part. Morgan still didn't know what John was feeling, if he felt anything at all. He pulled back the trigger on the pistol, never taking his eyes off her. Morgan supposed all this transpired in a few seconds, a couple of minutes at most, but it seemed hours that they stood there. None of it seemed real to her. She felt like she was floating above the scene, watching. Morgan was totally detached from what was happening.

Finally, John spoke, "Understand this, Morgan. I owe you nothing. Go away." He lowered his pistol, got in his truck, and drove away, leaving her there. Morgan never spoke to him again.

CHAPTER 10

Daniel Jacobs slammed down the receiver of his telephone. Now the damned FBI was calling. The whole situation was getting screwed up, and Lucas Brown was going to have all of them in jail on conspiracy and murder charges if he didn't fix this. He only had four more years until he could retire, and he didn't intend to let Lucas, or anyone else for that matter, screw up his retirement. He dialed Lucas's cell phone number.

"Hello?"

"Lucas, we've got a situation here. The Feds are calling, asking questions about her. You've got to back off."

"What do you mean asking questions? What kinds of questions?"

"They knew she had called me about that Gray thing. I denied it, said I had never heard of her and didn't know anything about it, but they were right on the mark. We're going to have to start answering questions here, man."

"The hell we are! You do what I told you to do. Nothing's changed. Find her! The Feds can't have her, or we would have gotten confirmation now. They'd have to turn her over. You know what to do." Lucas paced around his office. His office, like most others in town, was deserted. No one in the middle of the state was working today, it seemed, because of the snow. *Just another excuse for a day off,* Lucas mused. Things were getting messy. *How,* he wondered, *could one woman ever cause so much trouble?* This was, after all, a matter of national security, and one divorced thirtysomething woman who fooled around with an old police chief was at the heart of the matter. Really, the situation defied explanation. The situation infuriated Lucas. He'd have to step up the intensity.

CHAPTER 11

Morgan heard Frank's phone ring. It was answered immediately, she assumed, because it didn't ring again. A few moments later, Frank burst into the living room, grinning ear to ear. "I think we might be on to something here, my lady! A man from our office called the GBI and spoke with a Mr. Daniel Jacobs. He denied any knowledge of your phone call, said he had never spoken with you. He also denied any knowledge of the Randall Gray investigation. Jacobs was no help whatsoever, so we had the hotel pull the record of your calls from your room. And sure enough, you had called."

"Really? God, you think I'm standing here lying to you!" She smirked.

Frank rolled his eyes. "So our man called the day receptionist at her home, I might add, due to the snow, and she remembered your call quite well. She didn't remember your name, but she remembered you screaming about having seen a body and you couldn't tell the local authorities. She did remember transferring your call to Jacobs, though. Apparently, he's in the office more than the other agents are. And generally, he screens the calls and then decides who, if anyone, is to follow up. Jacob's denial is a good indicator that someone is covering something up. You're gaining credibility here, Morgan."

"Must be my lucky day."

"It just might be. Now I need you to tell me about the Kennedy thing again, from the beginning."

Once again, Morgan repeated the story John had told about the CIA, the Mafia, and John F. Kennedy. Via the internet, Frank and

Morgan looked up newspaper articles about the assassination. Frank had her scan the photos for familiar faces, maybe people she had seen in Clarkston or Williamstown. This proved to be useless. Morgan couldn't find anyone who looked familiar. More than forty years had passed since the photos were taken, and she wouldn't have recognized a picture of John from four decades earlier, much less someone who she had maybe seen walking around town a couple of times. She looked anyway; it seemed to make Frank happy.

Morgan didn't know it then, but a great deal more than she would have ever guessed was happening. Frank had spoken to his superiors and convinced them there was something to her story. Immediately, background checks and investigations were being done on anyone and everyone Morgan had mentioned. Military records were being pulled on John and company and everyone he had worked or associated with during the Vietnam War through the present. It was a massive undertaking with precious little time to be completed.

All the while, Morgan thought she was still trying to convince Frank of the legitimacy of her predicament. Frank thought he was still trying to convince his superiors the urgency of the situation. Truth of the matter was, Frank's boss was on the telephone with the justice department, getting permission for a massive operation that Morgan would never have imagined.

As the lunchtime news came on, once again Morgan was featured. Described as armed and dangerous, she was portrayed as an incredibly violent person to be feared by anyone she might meet. All Georgia residents were cautioned to immediately contact the authorities if she was seen. As Morgan stared at the television, she thought that this might possibly have been one of those situations that she would have found funny, if only it hadn't been so serious. A wave of despair swept over her, and once again her mind seemed to be numb. There was so much to think about, and she didn't have any answers to anything.

The local news finished up Morgan's story by declaring that several of her friends had been picked up for questioning and some had been charged with aiding and abetting a fugitive. Naturally, the ones charged were being held without bail. "I can't believe this crap! Those are my friends, and none of them even know anything about this! Can't you do something?"

"What would you have me do, Morgan? Would you like me to call Mr. Lucas Brown and tell him you're with me and all of this harassment just isn't necessary?" Frank laughed.

It infuriated Morgan. "Damn it! It's not fair! I want to go home, but I don't have a home. I want to see my kids, and I can't! I just want to leave!"

"Calm down, Morgan. If you leave, you're dead. I think we both can agree to that. I can't help you if you don't let me. I really do believe you, but I think what's wrong is that there's more to the story—either parts you haven't told me or parts you don't know. Might even be there's something you know that you don't think is important, but it might actually fit everything altogether. You've got to stay calm, and you've got to think. We'll get your friends out of jail. Nothing's going to happen to them."

"I don't imagine they'll be friends of mine by the time they get out."

Frank smiled and said, "Probably not, hon."

Great consolation that was. Later on, Morgan would find out that it wasn't just a couple of her friends that had been picked up for questioning. All friends—business associates, former employees, and distant relatives—were visited. Anyone who remotely seemed sympathetic to her was hauled off to the local police station in their area. The Clarkston residents, needless to say, were not treated very graciously. The roundup of Morgan's friends was due to Lucas and his friends getting fairly desperate to find her. Morgan thought it was good they were so busy because while everyone was occupied with gathering her acquaintances and helping people who were freezing in the snow, diligent FBI agents were converging on Clarkston. She was certain, though, that if this ever ended, there were going to be a lot of people really mad at her.

CHAPTER 12

Jacobs was still in the Atlanta office, waiting to hear again from Lucas, when the crew came in to work on the heating system in the GBI building. Apparently, he was too distracted by the current situation to bother asking them why they were working on a day when no one in the city was working. Two FBI agents, dressed as heating and air conditioning repairmen, walked right by his desk and proceeded, out of view, to put wiretaps on certain phones in the office. Simultaneously, agents who had arrived in Clarkston were installing listening devices near Lucas's home and office. The listening devices that were placed under the building structures worked fine, but the phone taps would prove to be disastrous. Morgan could have told the FBI that Lucas had the office and his home, she assumed, checked for bugs on a regular basis—usually twice a week. It only takes a few moments to do this with a little scanning device, and Lucas always believed in being thorough. However, nobody asked little Morgan anything, and she didn't know what was going on, so off they all headed on a terrible trip.

Morgan lay back down on the sofa. She assumed Frank was still in his bedroom on the telephone. She started to drift off to sleep and started thinking about a television show she had seen several years before. The show had been about a small-town police chief who had been asked to attend the electrocution of a convicted murderer. Unlike all the law enforcement people she currently knew, this police chief was opposed to the death penalty and did not wish to attend. The condemned man kept asking for him, and finally, the chief relented and went and visited the man in prison.

The prisoner had admitted what he had done and knew it was wrong. He had, however, been in prison for a very long time and in no way resembled the man he had been when first convicted. He explained, at length, to the police chief that the chief had been the only "good" man he had known when he was growing up and that he wanted the chief to be with him when he died. The chief couldn't find it in his heart to tell the man no, so he stayed through the electrocution. It was a heart-wrenching scene to watch.

The police chief returned home to his small town and was promptly asked by his deputies how the electrocution was and if he was all right. The chief's reply to that had been something to the effect of "The only humane way to kill a condemned man is to tell the man you're going to kill him and let him wait. Then right at the moment when you're going to pull the switch, you tell him he has been set free. As the condemned man stands and turns to walk away, you shoot him in the back of the head so he never knows what has happened."

As she drifted off to sleep, Morgan wondered if Frank was going to be like the police chief in the story—standing with her as she was hauled off to jail or watching as she was gunned down, going into a courthouse or some other equally gruesome ending to her life. The last conscious thought she had then was that she supposed Randall Gray would have been delighted to have thought he might actually escape the night he looked at her from her back porch. He hadn't been that lucky. Morgan was afraid she might not be as lucky as well.

Lucas Brown paced around his office. At least the snow was starting to melt. He was furious how basically an entire state was looking for Morgan, yet somehow, she had eluded everyone. She was either out of the state or holed up in a hotel. She damned sure wasn't with anyone they knew about; all those people were in jail or already questioned. Things were getting a little messy. He was going to have a good bit of explaining to do about the shake-up of her friends. There would be a lot of charges to be dropped later on. There was nothing to convict these people for—nothing to arrest them for—but at least now he knew she wasn't with them.

Something else was bothering Lucas too. Morgan had never gone anywhere without her kids. The obvious place to look was with people she knew, and that had not turned up anything. A lady with two little kids would have a hard time hiding for long without any help, but no one had seen them. It just didn't make sense.

All of a sudden, Lucas *did* know, and it all made perfect sense. Morgan was doing just the opposite of what she would normally do. This made her unpredictable and, therefore, more difficult to find. She would know how to do this because John would have told her that the most difficult person to catch is one who does everything backward. Right-handed people usually sit on the right-hand side of trains, buses, etc. If they are running and trying to escape, they always turn right. They don't think about it; it's instinct. Left-handed people always go left. Most escaped convicts are caught within thirty-six hours of leaving their cells because they can't resist calling their families, so consequently, one simply put taps on the home phones of family members. And within hours, the police knew right away where their suspect was. Usually, they could grab the escapee while he was still standing at the pay phone.

Now Lucas understood, and he laughed. He had made a mistake. He had assumed she'd run like anyone else, make the same stupid mistakes, and be caught rather quickly. Apparently, John had told her enough to at least make her difficult to catch. Lucas wondered how much she knew what to do—surely not much. He could just picture John and Morgan lying in bed together, discussing survival techniques after making love, and Lucas laughed so hard that he cried. Morgan might prove to be a challenge after all.

Lucas picked up the phone and called Jacobs. "Listen, call off the harassment. She's not with anyone."

"Are we calling the whole thing off, Lucas? I really don't like this," Jacobs replied.

"I don't care what you like. Do you realize what's at stake here? Do you know how many of us would take a fall if she told anyone even half of what I think she knows? You can kiss your fat retirement goodbye, my man, and spend your golden years behind bars with guys you had put there!"

"I know Lucas, but this is getting way out of hand. What is it you want us to do?"

"Start checking all the hotels, probably cheap ones. She's got to be somewhere. I don't think she's got the kids with her," Lucas said and hung up the phone. Lucas had killed John before the old man had told him what he wanted to know. He supposed John had loved her in some kind of way because he hadn't given up any information at all. Lucas needed something to do, so he decided to sweep the office for bugs. There weren't ever any around, but he found it fun, and it would give him something to do. Agitated and bored, he needed to keep busy.

The phone ringing again woke Morgan. She sat up on the sofa, trying to get her bearings. She was still tired and was beginning to wonder if she was always going to feel that way. Frank came running down the hall with a big grin on his face. "OK, Morgan! We got Brown on the phone with Jacobs. Jacobs isn't happy, and Brown sounds like he's starting to get worried because they can't find you. You've really pissed him off."

"Great! So now you can arrest them, and I can leave, right?" she asked.

"No, honey, not yet. This isn't as simple as all that. What we have is known as a situation. You're still charged with murder, and God only knows how many police officers are tied up in this thing with Brown. This is going take a little time."

"Well, while you guys are putting all the pieces together, I've done my part. And I want to see my kids. When can I leave?"

"I'm trying to see if I can get you in the witness protection program. If we can hide you and your girls out, all you have to do is wait. I should have an answer on that this afternoon. Except for the one phone call, we don't have much to go on, except for what you told us. I believe you, but me believing you and us being able to prove something are two different things. Hang in there."

Morgan didn't say anything. Yeah, she'd hang in there or just plain hang—she just wasn't sure which one it would be.

Lucas found the bug the FBI had planted at InterSecure. He didn't know who had put it there, but he was livid. He couldn't tell Robert because Robert would freak out and demand to know what was going on. He was already mad enough because Morgan had been charged with murder and said he just didn't believe it. That was one problem with Robert; he was so incorruptible. Everything was always simply right or wrong with him. Robert was another problem, though. Right now, the phone being tapped was a tremendous problem. It meant Morgan had help, and Lucas couldn't begin to comprehend who it might be. He called Jim on his cell phone and said nothing except for Jim to meet him immediately. Jim arrived about an hour later. Lucas explained the situation to him and demanded that Jim find out where the phone tap had come from. Jim left and made a few phone calls from a pay phone. It didn't take him too long to find out. When Jim returned, he was so amused he could hardly contain himself. "It's FBI, Lucas," Jim said, trying to not smile.

Lucas went crazy. He slung his arm across his desk, causing everything breakable to shatter on the floor and all the papers scattered. His face grew so contorted and red that Jim idly wondered if the man was going to literally have a stroke or heart attack then and there. He cursed, and he screamed. He kicked his chair. At that moment, it was hard for Jim to picture Lucas as the composed professional law enforcement officer he had been awarded for so many times over the years.

Finally, Jim laughed. He didn't intend to. One does not laugh at Lucas Brown, but Lucas was so out of control Jim couldn't help himself. Lucas heard the laugh and dove across his desk, shoving Jim up against the wall as he did. Lucas hit Jim repeatedly, breaking his nose and a couple of ribs before he stopped. "You're finished, Jim! I'm not covering for you anymore!" Lucas screamed.

Jim didn't say anything. Instead, he struggled to remain on his feet and wiped the blood from his face. He just shook his head and walked out the back door of the business. Jim would have to go to the hospital, but first, he was going to talk to Robert. It was time Robert knew what was going on.

Lucas left his office, stopped at the nearest pay phone, and made one quick call. A man answered the phone, and all Lucas said was "Find out what's going on." That was the entire conversation. Then he drove home. He wasn't surprised when he found the phones there had also been tapped. Lucas hadn't removed the bugs from his office because he didn't want them to know he was on to them. He figured he could actually give some false leads. Maybe the taps could be useful. He was still very agitated, though. He didn't like not being in control, and this whole situation was getting more complicated every hour. He paced around his living room, with a double shot of whiskey in a glass. Someone had better call him soon, or he was going to take over completely. Someone's head was going to roll over this.

Lucas's pager went off. He drove to the nearest pay phone and dialed the number.

"Hey, Lucas."

"Yeah, what's up?" Lucas asked.

"It's one of our guys. Frank Haggerty has her hidden somewhere, won't bring her in. Apparently, she was with him when you guys announced she had killed Henson. He's pushing pretty hard for her."

"Take care of this tonight," said Lucas.

"I can't do that, Lucas."

"Yes, you can, and you will. Why do I have to keep reminding you idiots what's at stake here! What has she told him?"

"Honest, Lucas. I don't know. I do know that everything's getting crazy up here."

"Why hasn't he turned her over?"

"He's her alibi for yesterday, and he won't give her up. Trying to get her in the witness program from what I hear."

"Then she's talked. Finish it tonight." And Lucas hung up the phone.

CHAPTER 13

Frank had ordered Chinese food for dinner that afternoon. They didn't watch the news because Frank said it made Morgan irritable. Periodically, he'd ask her a question, usually one he had already asked a thousand times before. And usually, she gave him the same answer. Morgan was starting to feel like they were an old married couple where their greatest joy in life was to nag each other. Morgan wanted to change the subject. "So do you miss her?" she asked.

"Miss who?"

"Your wife."

"Sure, I do. What's that got to do with anything?"

"Well, why don't you go get her back?"

"I doubt that she'd come. She grew tired of being an agent's wife."

"So you didn't love her enough to change jobs?"

"It wasn't something I could do at the time."

"I always thought it would be really fun to have someone care enough about me to give up something that was really important to them just for me. I don't think I'd ever ask them to give up anything, but it would be really neat to know that they would," Morgan said.

"Some things you just can't let go of, Morgan."

"It's still just a job, Frank."

"This wasn't about the job. I'd love to quit. Maybe soon." Frank didn't want to talk about his wife anymore.

Morgan could tell by the look in his eyes that he missed her. She found herself wondering if she'd cheated on him. Maybe she got tired of sitting up late at night, waiting for him to come home. Maybe she got tired of wondering *if* he'd come home every day from work. Morgan surmised it would be a pretty hard deal. "Can we go outside or something?" Morgan asked.

"It's freezing outside, and the snow's all slushy. Why do you want to go outside?"

"Because I'm tired of being inside, and it's getting dark. And I'd like to stretch my legs. No offense, but I'm getting real tired of your sofa here." Morgan smiled, and Frank laughed.

Frank got their coats, and they went out his back door. He had a small fenced backyard and a swimming pool that was covered for the winter. There were a couple of large oak trees farther down the yard, and one of the trees had an old tire swing hanging from a large limb. Morgan imagined his kids used to swing there, and he probably couldn't bring himself to take it down. The far back corner of the yard hosted a storage building or a workshop. Morgan couldn't tell which as it was getting fairly dark. They walked around the edge of the pool and talked.

"I still don't understand, Morgan. You're bright, and you're pretty, so how did you get messed up in all of this?" he asked.

"I really don't know. I guess I'm a sucker for a good line, and you've got to understand, most of this stuff I didn't believe anyway. Then everything just started snowballing, and I couldn't seem to make it stop."

"Did you ever just think about leaving, maybe after the first couple of break-ins at the skating rink?"

"Yeah, but I really didn't associate the break-ins with John or Lucas. I got mad because I knew the police could have done a lot more if they had wanted to. But I just figured it was a small town, and they just didn't care. It took me a while—about up to the time people started dying—to assume all of this was connected." Just as Morgan was finishing her sentence, a pair of headlights swung around the corner of the street and into Frank's driveway. "Are you expecting someone?" she asked.

"No, and be quiet!" Frank said and grabbed her arm and pulled her up against the back outside wall of his house. Immediately, they heard something breaking—either his front bay window or the glass windowpane in his front door. The initial crash was followed by machine-gun fire. Morgan stood there idiotically and briefly thought that all the little flashes of fire coming from the guns would be kind of pretty under different circumstances. Probably, she was not as bright as Frank thought she was. Morgan almost laughed at the stupidity of it all.

As the windows in the back of the house started breaking, Frank shoved Morgan down to the ground, and they crawled over the edge of the pool. "Get down in there!" He pointed. What he wanted Morgan to do was to crawl under the pool cover and hide in the pool. She didn't find this a very attractive idea as it was freezing outside. She had no clue as to whether or not he had drained his pool before covering it, and she had no way of knowing what else might be in there. Morgan hesitated about a second but jumped in quickly when the bullets started flying past them. Morgan fell in the pool, with Frank tumbling down behind her. It was absolutely horrible. Naturally, when she had jumped in, she hadn't managed to land feet first, falling instead sideways and landing on her arm, closely followed by her face. There was, she guessed, about eight to ten inches of water in the bottom of the pool. It was incredibly cold and pitch-black. The only thing Morgan could see was the smoke from their breath coming out in quick little puffs.

Frank reached out and whispered, "Don't make a sound. I guess they didn't hear us with all the gunfire. Whatever you do, no noise!"

Morgan nodded but was sure he couldn't see it. They heard a door open and heard footsteps. Morgan assumed the feet belonged to the same people who had just riddled Frank's house with gunfire. Morgan also assumed they were looking for the two of them.

"Dammit! Where are they?" asked one.

"The car's in the garage. They've got to be here!"

"Damn! They're not here. Brown's going to crack up. Let's get out of here."

"We haven't found them. What are we supposed to do?"

"Look, the street cops are going to be here in about three more minutes. We've got to go, unless you want to explain what we're doing."

The police did come. And they stayed. For six hours, they investigated whatever it was they thought they had found. For six hours, Frank and

Morgan huddled together in the shallow end of the pool, trying not to freeze to death. For six hours, they listened to the cops discuss the evidence, look for more, and discuss where Frank and Morgan might be. Some even suggested that maybe he had lost his mind as he seemed to be harboring a fugitive. They couldn't get out of the pool because the police would have taken Morgan into custody. Neither Frank nor Morgan mentioned it, but they both knew, given the circumstances, that she would somehow be killed if she were arrested. Morgan sat there in the freezing water and wondered how people trapped in avalanches ever survived until a rescue team showed up. She had never been so cold in her life.

Finally, around 6:00 a.m., the policemen left. Morgan couldn't remember ever being so grateful for anything in her life. When he was sure they had gone, Frank managed to pull himself out of the pool, leaving Morgan there while he went to the front of the house to see if they had left anyone to guard his home. A few minutes later, he came back, saying no one was there then, but he was sure they would be back at dawn to search for more clues as the sun came up. The cold had worked in their favor as, apparently, none of the policemen had really wanted to stay outside any longer than necessary. Morgan could relate to that. Morgan tried to get out of the pool but couldn't. She was stiff and frozen and unable to move. Frank basically lifted her out and dragged her into his house.

The house was a disaster. Everything was broken, with shattered glass all over. It was impossible to take a step without hearing the glass crunch underneath the soles of their shoes. The furniture was thrown about, with huge holes in the fabric and with stuffing working its way out. Pictures were ruined, memories and mementos destroyed. Morgan felt like she had stepped into a war zone. "I'm so sorry, Frank" was all she could manage to whisper.

"C'mon, Morgan. We've got to get moving. They'll be back."

"I can't move, Frank. I'm too cold."

"You've got to move, and we've got to go."

"Where are we going?"

"I don't know yet. We've got a new problem. I'll tell you in the car."

A new problem wasn't exactly what Morgan needed. She couldn't imagine a new problem. Hell, she couldn't imagine the old problem, and now he said they have another one. Morgan opened her mouth to express her opinion, but he grabbed her by the arm again and led her to the car. Once inside the vehicle, he told her to lie down on the back seat and under no circumstances was she to raise her head. It didn't seem like a bad idea to Morgan.

Once they were out of his little subdivision, Frank turned the headlights and the heat on as high as it would go. Morgan desperately needed something to cover up with as she had never been remotely close to this cold in her life. She was lying in the back seat, curled up and shivering. Frank asked if she was all right, and she muttered something before drifting off into a different place.

Morgan is with John once again, and they are happy. John is holding her in his arms, and she feels safe. His face has an expression of pure love on it, and he is rubbing her cheek with the back of his hand. Morgan's children are playing in the same room, and occasionally, he would look at them and laugh. The four of them eat supper in the living room, on the sofa, with John feeding Morgan most of the time. When her daughters need something, he'd get it for them. There is a fire burning in the fireplace, and a soft glow illuminates from the hearth. Morgan feels incredibly happy.

The evening grows old, and it's the girl's bedtime. John says he'll put them to bed, so they give Morgan kisses and hugs and run upstairs to beat John to their bedroom. John leans down over the sofa and gives her a very soft, tender, passionate kiss. He tells her he'll be right back, and their evening can start. Morgan knows what he means. Once her daughters are sound asleep, they're going to make love in front of the fireplace. It is always one of their favorite spots. John turns and walks upstairs.

Morgan lays a quilt on the floor in front of the fireplace. She pours some wine in two long-stemmed glasses. She looks out the window and sees that it has begun to snow. Morgan thinks it will be their first time to make love while it's snowing. She hears John's footsteps coming down the stairs, and she smiles.

The living room lights are dimmed, so there is not much light, except for the glow from the flames in the fireplace. Morgan puts another log on the fire, and John comes up behind her before she can turn around. He wraps his arms around her waist and kisses her neck. His hands grope for the buttons on her blouse, and he begins undressing her. She is totally enthralled with what's happening, but she realizes something is wrong. Something doesn't feel right, and his hands feel sticky against her skin. Morgan turns around to look at him. He's covered in blood and has a horrible contorted look on his face, but he's grinning. The reflection from the fireplace shines from his eyes, and his lips curl up from his teeth as he grins even bigger. He reaches out for her. Morgan can't move and still don't understand what's happened.

He grabs her by the hair and bends her head backward. Everything seems to be happening in slow-motion. John laughs and pulls a large switchblade knife from his pocket. As he puts the blade against her throat, he says, "This won't hurt at all. Your children never felt a thing. You should be happy for them."

Then Morgan knows what has happened. The sticky blood is from her children, presumably lying upstairs somewhere—dead. Morgan doesn't care if he kills her, but she does want to see her children. Morgan tries to break free from his grasp, all the while picturing what the scene upstairs will entail. She struggles, hitting and kicking him, but can get nowhere. All the while, he just keeps laughing. He's still laughing as he begins sliding the blade across her throat...

Morgan jerked up in the back seat of Frank's car. It took her a few moments to realize where she was. Frank asked if she was doing all right. "I'm losing my mind" was her answer.

CHAPTER 14

Only a few minutes passed between the time the lynch mob left Frank's house and when Lucas found out, apparently, that no one had been home. Communication had been somewhat slowed by the bugs on the phones, but all that was required was a page and a quick drive to a nearby pay phone. Lucas hadn't taken the news well at all, and his reply had been a long string of profanities. Now he was getting seriously worried.

Before he had time to leave the phone booth, his pager had beeped again. Lucas had been hoping he wouldn't ever receive this page, but he also knew the situation had progressed to the point where he had expected the page to come. Lucas dialed the number, and when the receiver was answered on the other end of the line, Lucas was given quick instructions on where to go for a meeting and debriefing. Lucas never said a word. He knew there wasn't anything to say.

Frank drove without saying anything else until just before the sun came up. Morgan knew they were somewhere in the northern part of Georgia but wasn't sure where. As she had begun to thaw out in the car, her arm had begun to hurt badly. Morgan assumed she had been too scared or too cold in the pool to notice, but when she had jumped in the pool, apparently, she had hurt her wrist. There was a fair-sized lump with a lot of bruising around it. She wondered vaguely if her arm was broken, but it really didn't seem all that important at the time. "Frank?" she asked.

"Yeah?"

"I know this isn't really important, but I could really use a cup of coffee and some cigarettes, not to mention some dry clothes."

"Give me about ten more minutes, and I'll be more than happy to accommodate you, my dear."

"Always the gentleman. I don't think I would have ever left you."

"I'm an ass to live with. You've just gotten the professional side of me." Frank made a face and then grinned at Morgan.

Frank pulled into the parking lot of a small fairly run-down hotel. Morgan sat in the car as he went in. He must have awakened the owner or manager because the man who came up to the front desk did not appear too happy. Morgan couldn't hear what was said as she was still in the car, but there seemed to be a fairly angry exchange of words, with Frank obviously getting the better of the conversation.

He emerged victorious, room key in hand, and trotted back to the car. "OK, now let's get you inside, and I've got to hide the car."

Frank showed Morgan which room was theirs, and she unlocked the door as he drove off in the car. The room was quite unremarkable, with two double beds separated by a small nightstand. There was an ancient telephone on the nightstand. Across the room was a small black-and-white television set sitting upon a table that resembled a crate. A small lamp sat on the table beside the television. The bathroom was about three decades out of date, complete with the toilet that wouldn't stop running, even when Morgan jiggled the handle. For a finishing touch, all this was covered with about an inch of dust, but the whole thing felt like the Ritz-Carlton to her. She couldn't have been happier.

Frank came through the door a few minutes later, bolting through it. He had a bag with him, which contained—to Morgan's ultimate delight—three packs of cigarettes and two cups of coffee. Then he moved the crate and television set by the door, just in case they might need a couple of extra minutes to escape. There wasn't a back door to this fine establishment for one to escape through, but Morgan decided not to argue the point.

Morgan sat down on the edge of the bed and slipped her coat off. It was still damp, and she found herself shivering profusely. She wasn't sure though if she was cold or scared or maybe it was even because of her arm. It didn't seem to matter at the time. She sipped the coffee and lit a cigarette. Morgan had never had anything that tasted so good in her life. Frank sat and sipped his coffee and smoked a cigarette too. He was watching her but not saying anything. Morgan supposed he was trying to see how well she was holding up under the strain.

I could tell you, Frank, Morgan thought. *I'm not holding up worth a damn. This is all beyond me. I do not want to play this game. I don't want to be here. I don't like these people. I want to be left alone.* Instead, all she said was "Frank, I need a little help, please."

"What is it?"

"I really want to go soak in the tub and try to warm up. But I can't move my wrist, and I can't get undressed." She was terribly embarrassed after she said it, but at the time, she couldn't think of any reason to stay out the tub. A "last bath" if you will.

"What's wrong with your wrist?" he asked.

"I don't know. I guess I sprained it jumping into the pool," she said and held out her arm.

Frank grimaced when he saw the lump. "Why didn't you say something?"

"And what would you have done? Would you have hopped out of the pool and asked the nice gentlemen with the machine guns if they could please stop shooting long enough for you to take care of my arm?"

"You're a smart-ass, Morgan. As a matter of fact, I don't understand you at all. You've seen a murder, you're charged with a murder, you've sat in a pool for hours in freezing weather, and you haven't commented on it at all. Are you OK?"

Was she OK? Now she was wondering if *he* was OK. No, she was not all right. Morgan was beyond scared, beyond terrified. Her arm hurt terribly, and she was still cold. She didn't think she was ever going to get warm. People were shooting at her. And from her perspective, she wasn't in much better shape now—having met Frank—than she was before she decided to try to talk to someone. What was there to say? Truth of the matter was, she was desperately trying to maintain some semblance of composure. Morgan knew if she let herself cry or scream, she probably would not be able to stop, maybe ever. Morgan feared losing her sanity almost as much as she feared being killed, probably more. She simply could not afford the luxury of allowing herself to get upset.

Responding to Frank's question, Morgan just shrugged.

Ever the gentleman, Frank did help her undress, politely looking away as he did. He ran the bathwater for her and announced he was going out to get something to wrap her arm with. Morgan slid into the tub, and slowly, her body temperature began to rise. It felt wonderful. For a couple of blissful minutes, she didn't think about anything—no Lucas Brown, no murders, no Kennedy assassination, no John. It was pure, unadulterated relief.

This peace lasted maybe a minute, and then the reality of the situation flooded her mind, like a tidal wave washing over her. The water in the tub was quite warm, but Morgan suddenly felt chilled again, and she began shivering. Morgan imagined noises by the door, fearing someone knew where they had gone. Morgan was afraid to get out of the tub, terrified of opening the bathroom door. She began breathing fast and felt like she was going to faint. She wrapped her arms around herself and tried to control the shaking. Finally, thankfully, the shaking subsided somewhat, and Morgan was able to slow her breathing. She crawled, literally, out of the tub and knelt on the floor. She envisioned all types of scenarios upon opening the bathroom door, none of them good. She couldn't possibly fight off anyone. She couldn't pick up a pencil at the time, much less hit someone or try to fight them off. The fear, hopelessness, and despair paralyzed her. Finally, she decided that it didn't matter anyway because she couldn't have ever fought anyone off her anyway. Her mind raced. She never thought she would have been this scared just because Frank had left for a few minutes. She felt totally helpless.

Morgan leaned up against the bathroom door. She tried to tell herself she was being silly—no one could possibly have known where he or she was. Of course, no one was supposed to know they had been at Frank's house either, and that had not certainly turned out well. The pool experience was not in her top ten of most enjoyable evenings.

She heard the hotel door shut. She heard a man's voice but couldn't understand what he was saying. She couldn't make out the voice. Morgan wanted to call Frank's name but couldn't. The doorknob started turning on the bathroom door. She was terrified. She was shaking so badly she couldn't stand any longer and sat down on the floor next to the tub. The door began to open; it seemed to open very slowly.

The whole scene was really quite eerie. The steam from the bathtub began flowing out the door as it opened. The bathroom mirror was steamed up, so all Morgan could see was a vague shadow of a hand coming through the door opening. The body emerged through the door. She tried to scream but couldn't. Morgan wanted to hide, but where does one hide in a bathroom? Just as she was sure she was going to die at the hands of Lucas Brown himself, Morgan looked up and saw a pair of hands and arms reaching down toward her. Blame the fear, the arm, the pool deal, or exhaustion. Morgan didn't know which one was to blame, not that it mattered, but she fainted. Morgan didn't know if one could dream or have nightmares or hallucinations when one had fainted. If one could, she did. If it was not possible, she had no explanation, but she would remember clearly what was in her mind.

Morgan finds herself at Martha's Vineyard with the Kennedy clan. All of them are there—John and Bobby, John Jr., Ted, etc. They all look exactly as Morgan had seen photos of them in magazines and history books in high school and college. John F. Kennedy, Jackie, John Jr., and Caroline all sit around a patio table by the pool. Ted Kennedy is strolling around the pool with his latest mistress. Bobby is standing, drink in hand, discussing his appointment for the attorney general of the United States.

This, of course, was insanity in itself. Morgan was dreaming of attending a party composed mostly of dead people. JFK and Bobby had, of course, been assassinated decades before. Jackie had recently died from a prolonged illness. John Jr., his lovely wife, and her sister had more recently died in a tragic plane crash, presumably an accident of John Jr.'s own making.

Through the haze of the dream, Morgan is standing on the far side of the lawn, just watching. She can't tell if the Kennedys can see her or not. She finds herself momentarily caught up in the tragedy of the whole Kennedy scene, wondering why a family, any family, would have to endure so many tragic deaths. Surely, one murder, one battle with a terminal disease, or one accidental tragic death would be enough for any family to have to endure for several generations, let alone every few years.

"You really shouldn't be so sentimental, Morgan," she hears John say as his arms slide around her waist. He is standing behind her, hugging her tightly. He leans over and kisses the back of her neck, something Morgan has always loved for him to do. "You know, honey," he says, "everybody has a cross to bear in life. In this case, they just have a heavier cross than most. Anyway, show me a person who doesn't have any problems in life, and I'll show you someone who will die young. You either live a short, carefree life or endure years of endless suffering. It's just the way of things."

"The way of what things? Why does it have to be like that?" she asks.

"Just because it does," says Lucas Brown.

Morgan swings around in John's arms, startled. John laughs, and Lucas has a huge grin on his face.

"You don't understand," says Lucas, "the way of the world. Some things just *have* to be. It doesn't matter at all if it's right or wrong. It doesn't matter if you agree with it or not. It's just what happens. You really take all of this much too personally."

"Well," Morgan replies, "what if we go over there and just tell them if they don't go to the places they were killed, maybe it will turn out differently?" Brilliant statement, she knows, but it is the best she can do at the time.

"It wouldn't matter," John says.

"We'd kill them anyway," Lucas says.

"What do you mean we'd kill them anyway?" she asks.

"Baby," John explains, "I told you over and over. That's what we do. It's just legal when we do it." He hugs Morgan tighter.

"No!" Morgan screams. "It's not right."

"Remember, Morgan, it doesn't matter if it's right or wrong. That doesn't have anything to do with it. Deals are made, and deals have to be kept. One would lose all credibility if one did not keep up his end of the bargain," says Lucas as he begins loading a rifle.

"John, please do something," she begs.

"I am, honey. I'm going to help." With that said, John and Lucas start methodically aiming at the Kennedys. One at a time, the Kennedys fall to the ground. Morgan runs across the lawn, screaming for them to run, to go hide. Bullets, one at a time, fly past her head. Each time one does, another Kennedy falls to the ground a fraction of a second later. Blood is spewing everywhere. The glass Bobby is holding shatters as it falls from his hand as he hits the ground.

Morgan keeps yelling for them to move, run inside, but no one would move. It's like they are resigned to their fate and understood that running and hiding will be useless.

"You can't change fate, Morgan," she hears John say from the other side of the lawn. "You'll end up the same, but you'll try to hide. You're so damned stubborn sometimes."

"But why me?" she asks.

"Because I told you too much and just because it has to be," he answers.

"Don't take it so personal," says Lucas as he raises his rifle for his final shot—the shot he'll fire at Morgan.

Thankfully, the dream ended. Morgan awoke long enough to realize she was lying on a bed, covered with the bedspread, with Frank doing something to her arm. He smiled at her, said everything was all right, and handed her a pill. He said it would help subdue the pain.

Paranoia is a strange thing. It can distort one's ability to rationalize anything. One loses all common sense and cannot distinguish fact from fiction. Morgan was rapidly approaching this point and was trying desperately to stay calm, telling herself that Frank was the one who had been trying to help—although she wasn't at all certain one could call the most recent events helpful.

As he held her head so she could take a sip of water and swallow the pill, she remembered thinking that he was probably poisoning her and this would be the end of her life. Morgan had no sound reason for feeling this way, but then again, she wasn't exactly in a sound situation either. Through blurry eyes, she watched his face as he stared at her as she swallowed the pill. She tried to say something, but no words would come, so she simply lay back on the pillow and drifted off. The dreams came in rapid succession—a seemingly never-ending succession of nightmares of violence, plots, and murders.

CHAPTER 15

Robert listened to Jim as he drove him to the hospital. They had already talked for a great while, and it had become obvious Lucas had at least broken a few of Jim's ribs and maybe caused some internal bleeding. Robert was trying to remain calm. It was no secret that Jim and Lucas didn't like each other, but the things Jim was saying went well beyond a simple dislike for someone.

There were also some very serious ramifications of what Jim was saying. First, the business Robert and Lucas had struggled to build for so long would immediately lose all credibility if any of Jim's stories were true. Secondly, Lucas would be guilty of several major felonies, and Robert doubted very seriously if he had enough clout to get this covered up. Third, he knew Morgan definitely was not a murderer, and he had been disturbed earlier when Lucas had seemed so pleased that she had been charged with John's murder. Robert hadn't understood that at all, but sometimes, he knew Lucas took great pleasure in other people's trouble.

Naturally though, there seemed to be a problem with Jim's story too. All Jim knew was that Lucas was crazy and frequently broke the law or got others to do it for him to get what he wanted. Jim didn't know why. Robert didn't know why Lucas did the things he did. The only motive the two of them could come up with was some sort of sick vendetta, but even that seemed to be reaching. Why would Lucas risk so much just to get even with someone? And what in God's name could Morgan, of all people, have done to warrant such uncontrolled rage? Robert couldn't figure it out, but he knew he had to talk to Lucas. Maybe he could get some answers from him. The whole mess was making Robert very tense, and he could feel the early beginnings of a migraine coming on. He felt very tired all of a sudden.

There is a very common public misconception that law enforcement officers all hate a crooked cop. This really isn't true. Policemen share a bond—sometimes real and sometimes imagined—that they're up against the world, a sordid society that is out to lie, cheat, steal, and murder at any available opportunity. To this end, each law enforcement agency has a fierce loyalty to its own, and this same loyalty spreads out through other affiliated agencies. Occasionally, a rift may occur over some jurisdictional discrepancy. But overall, the general mode of operation is to protect their own kind over and above anything else.

Also, many high-ranking federal agents either begin their careers in the military or as local police officers or have somehow worked their way up to higher levels and higher agencies. The result of these promotions in rank eventually will lead to a very tight-knit group of officers spreading through all divisions of the various law enforcement agencies. For instance, a dedicated street cop can possibly work his way out of the local jurisdiction and begin working for the Georgia Bureau of Investigation. Once he has attained this level, he begins making associates at higher levels of law enforcement, such as the Federal Bureau of Investigation.

Consequently, should some lowly policeman need a helping hand, he simply calls his old friend who got promoted to the Georgia Bureau of Investigation and asks for assistance. Should the friend not be able to help, he picks up the phone and calls his new friends in the Federal Bureau of Investigation. Eventually, someone is found who can assist the policeman with his dilemma. This process is frequently referred to as the good ol' boy system in Georgia and is as prevalent in politics as it is in law enforcement. Connections are everything in Georgia. Guilt and innocence don't mean anything. There are also exceptions to every rule.

Jim and Robert both were basically good, dedicated officers. Both had done their share of ticket fixing and sometimes just turning their heads, but mostly, they honestly believed in the system. Both of them had discussed problems with judges before cases had been heard to help the outcome, but it had always been for a friend, so it was a worthy cause. John had regularly visited the Clarkston judges before trials and always got the outcome he had anticipated. These things weren't considered wrong in Georgia—just the way things were done.

There is another unspoken rule among law enforcement agents: one is never to hurt, in any way, another officer. Lucas had crossed that line with Jim and, from Robert's viewpoint, also with him. Lucas had put their reputations on the line and their business at risk. Robert was certain there would be many long discussions regarding these matters. Robert tried to call Lucas after Jim had been admitted to the emergency room but to no avail. Lucas wasn't at work, wasn't at home, and wasn't answering his cell phone. Lucas was adamant about being kept in the know about everything, so Robert also found this very strange. Robert slammed down the pay phone in the hospital waiting room and reached behind his head to rub his neck. His headache was getting much worse.

Lucas had left early for his prearranged meeting. It had taken him nearly two hours to lose the federal agents that were following him. He had stopped by the post office, the bank, and the grocery store—all to no avail. A couple of times, they had switched out. And for a few minutes, he wasn't sure which car was tailing him. But never to be defeated, Lucas had persevered and had managed to elude them. He actually found it somewhat amusing that they had the audacity to think they could actually keep up with him. After all, he had at least participated in the planning stages of almost all the major training manuals for most of the law enforcement agencies. He knew all the tricks, and he had all the skills. He was, after all, Lucas Brown.

There was one battle brewing that Lucas hadn't counted on. He had not anticipated how angry the FBI would become from the raid on Frank's home. Lucas had floated the rumor about Frank crossing over and hiding a fugitive, and he had assumed that it would suffice. Frank, however, had been with the Federal Bureau of Investigation for years and had made many friends during this time—friends who were angry that anyone, even Lucas the Great, would have the nerve to try to attack his home and his reputation. Policemen, of any sort, take great offense at their homes being vandalized as they feel they shouldn't be subject to such violations. Lucas's rumor had worked fine for the locals, but the Feds that were beginning to ascend upon Georgia weren't so quick to buy the story.

The problem with the human race is, they tend to rationalize and justify all they do. Any misdeed or sin can be rectified by some sort of excuse. Unfortunately, Morgan decided she was no different. She was sure she did some things terribly wrong. Certain she was responsible for Randall Gray's death, she tried to make herself feel better by saying she didn't know he would die. Morgan didn't really think anyone would hurt him. How could she have known? Ultimately, she was responsible for John's death too, but she tried to tell herself it wasn't her that killed him, that it couldn't be her fault. Morgan never asked John to tell her all the crap that he did. She never wanted to know. Maybe she was guilty of nothing, except being naive. Knowing this made it all the easier to handle. Problem was, she couldn't even convince herself any of this was true.

Morgan dreamed about murders, assassinations, and government conspiracies. She dreamed of judges sentencing innocent people to die in Georgia's electric chair for crimes of which they had no part. She dreamed again of Randall Gray on her porch, pleading with his eyes for her to help him. She had the reoccurring dream of John killing her children with his knife while he was supposed to be tucking them in bed. Morgan even dreamed that she purposefully killed John. It was a really strange dream because in this one, Morgan intentionally hurt someone, something she had never done in her life.

John and Morgan are standing in some sort of tunnel. It's really dark, but at the far end of the tunnel, there's a bright light shining. There's fog all around them, and there's a thick mist in the air. They both seem to be moving in slow-motion. Morgan tells John she wants to go with him; she doesn't want to be left alone any longer. He laughs at her and tells her he's going to the other end of the tunnel, but she can't go. Morgan asks why, and he says because he can't stand the sight of her any longer. Morgan goes crazy and starts screaming for him to stop, that he has to take her with him, but he just laughs. The angrier she becomes, the harder he laughs. Eventually, all Morgan can hear is him laughing at her.

He turns and begins walking to the end of the tunnel, still laughing. What a joke she's been to him! Morgan tries to run after him, but she can't move. She looks down at her hands and sees that she has a pistol. John is still laughing as she raises her arm and aims the gun at him. He doesn't know because he's walking away from her, but Morgan guesses he hears her pull the hammer of the pistol back because as the hammer clicks into place, he stops walking. Morgan waits for him to turn around, but he doesn't do this. He did quit laughing though. Morgan fires the pistol. As the gun explodes, it gives off an eerie glow in the dark tunnel. She's surprised when John screams. She's even more surprised that she actually hit his leg. John falls down, grasping at his leg. He screams a long line of profanities, which Morgan ignores. She walks down the tunnel until she's standing over him. Morgan tells him she bets he now wishes he had taken her with him, but instead of agreeing, he starts the damned laughing again. He laughs and laughs with tears streaming down his face. He's still laughing as she aims the gun at him again. Once again, she pulls back the hammer. He keeps on laughing. Morgan doesn't really want to kill him, but he just won't stop the laughing. She aims the gun directly at his chest, right where she thinks his heart should be. He keeps on laughing. Again Morgan pulls the trigger. This time, she is close enough to see flesh rip open and the blood spew out. Blood spurts on her, seemingly with the very beating of his heart. Morgan is shocked at what she has done, but at least, he doesn't scream this time. He just laughs. She kneels down beside him and just looks. She watches as the blood continues to rhythmically pump out of his body. He keeps on laughing, but as he loses more blood, the laughter grows softer, something Morgan is eternally grateful for at the time. He's still quietly laughing as he takes his last breath...

Later on, Morgan would remember thinking that this dream was probably some sort of a very poor psychological ploy on behalf of her weary brain to try to even the score. Perhaps somewhere in her subconscious, she believed that if she could kill one of them, it would end her current situation. Morgan didn't know. The only truth she had about the dream was once again she woke with a start, covered in sweat and shaking profoundly. Once again, she was convinced she was going insane.

CHAPTER 16

Lucas finally made it to his rendezvous undetected. He was rather pleased with himself for that accomplishment, but he also knew this meeting wasn't going to be pleasant. His main goal currently was simply damage control. Surely, Lucas could lie his way out of this. There was no way that a woman was going to ruin his career. Lucas collected his thoughts and turned off his car. The snow had begun to melt slightly, but it was still rather cold. He was at an abandoned airport hangar on the old side of the Hartsfield-Jackson Atlanta International Airport. The only people that ever showed up in this area of the airport were an occasional maintenance man or a bored security guard. Neither would pose a problem for Lucas should they happen to stop by at an inopportune time.

Lucas got out of his car, buttoned his overcoat, and walked into the hangar. He was not surprised to see three men standing in the middle of the hangar, waiting for him. The two gentlemen on each side of the middle man were just agents, but the man in the middle was the assistant deputy director of the CIA. Lucas and he were old friends, but no pleasantries were going to be exchanged this time.

The deputy director was wearing black slacks and a black overcoat. He had on a pair of sunglasses, which were totally unnecessary, and a Stetson hat tilted forward to help conceal his identity. Lucas couldn't see his expression, but as soon as he spoke, Lucas knew by the tone of his voice that he was not very pleased.

"Brown, we have been more than lenient in our rein with you. Can you please tell me how you have managed to screw up so badly? How in the hell could you kill Henson and blame some girl that was with an FBI agent at the time of the murder? Didn't it occur to you that someone just might not believe she could be in two places at once?"

"Sir, her whereabouts were believed to be elsewhere at the time. And we, I, assumed there would be no problem in framing her for the murder. Once she is in custody, it wouldn't be any problem to be rid of the problem."

"Why hasn't this FBI Agent Haggarty turned her over? Why does he consider this a federal matter?"

"I'm not sure, but he hasn't returned to work. And we haven't been able to pinpoint their location yet. I'm certain they will be found in a matter of hours, sir."

"How much does she know, Lucas?"

"Henson said she knew everything. The old son of a bitch had a thing for her, and I guess he got a conscience as he was getting older. Even when I had ordered him to kill her, he didn't do it. That's why I disposed of him."

"Washington is going to restructure the plan. You have two days to find her and eliminate both the girl and this Agent Haggarty. Then you and your family and several other key people will be relocated. You've created a hell of a mess, Lucas."

"I created nothing! The bastard opened his mouth and told three decades of secrets. What in the hell was I supposed to do about that?"

"You were in charge of the operation, Lucas. You have failed miserably. Complacency is a very dangerous attribute. We'll talk more when this is finished. Meanwhile, clean this up. It's getting messy. It's your responsibility, and the consequences are quite grave. There are some things the public just cannot ever know. Do you understand?"

"Yes, sir" was all Lucas could say.

The three men turned and walked out of the hangar. Lucas was so angry he couldn't think clearly. All he knew was that he would kill Morgan himself. His whole career wasn't going to be destroyed by her. As he was standing there in the hangar, watching his breath hang in the cold air and trying to regain his composure, he finally realized why Haggarty hadn't turned her over. "Damn," he said and walked to his car.

Lucas used his cell phone to call Dan Jacobs. He told him to run a background check on Frank Haggarty, just to make sure he was who Lucas thought he was.

"Lucas, it's really getting bad around here. Everyone is asking questions, and I don't have answers for them. Can't we just let this die? Eventually, Haggarty is going to have to hand her over. And when he does, you can take care of her."

"By the time he hands her over, there won't be anything left to take care of you, asshole," Lucas replied. "Now just do it and call me right back!"

"All right." Jacobs sighed, and he began punching keys on his computer. Jacobs intended to get the report for Lucas and then go home. He was tired. He was also sure he would probably never be employed long enough to get his pension now. He was beginning to wonder what in the hell he was going to do.

Lucas then called his house. He knew his wife and son would be at her mother's house, but he also knew the phone lines were tapped, which was the reason for the call. The answering machine picked up on the fourth ring, and Lucas waited patiently for the beep that signaled he could leave his message. "Hi, hon, I'm going to the condo on the beach for a couple of days to try to catch up on some paperwork. I tried Robert, couldn't get through, so give him a call for me, please. I guess the phone lines are frozen. I've been trying to call you all day. Love you and the little guy. Be home in a couple of days. Bye, hon."

Lucas really didn't have any idea if he would ever go home again or not. He supposed it would all depend on how much damage control he could do after he killed Morgan. Naturally, he couldn't determine the damage until he talked to her and figured out how much she really knew and how much she had told and to whom it had been told. It really didn't matter all that much though because either way, Lucas was sure he could straighten things out. After all, there were really only two scenarios: The first was that he would kill Morgan after he was certain that she hadn't really figured out anything, which was most probable, and he would return home. Sure, there would be a lot of questions asked, but phone calls would be made from Washington to Georgia. Certain people would be told to stop asking questions, and after a few days, it would all die down. After all, Morgan certainly wasn't important, and her parents are dead, so there wouldn't be anyone to ask a lot of questions on her behalf. Lucas knew he had to find her kids, though. Naturally, they were going to have to disappear too, just so they couldn't cause any problems later. No big deal. The second scenario Lucas wasn't real pleased about, but it would be functional if necessary. The powers that be might still be slightly irritated and decide Lucas needed to be transferred. He was sure he would be relocated to Washington, if this turned out to be true. He would probably just never go home, leaving his wife and son to wonder what had happened to him. Later they would receive a settlement from the government, have plenty of money to live on, and probably never think of him again. Lucas decided either scenario wouldn't be so bad. Family life was a pain in the butt sometimes, so he wouldn't mind leaving. But on the other hand, he had been there for quite a while now and had grown accustomed to the routine.

Either way, it really didn't matter to Lucas. All he had to do was get rid of Morgan, and the rest would simply fall into place. Lucas was deep in thought when his cell phone rang. It was Dan Jacobs with the background on Frank. "Read it to me," said Lucas.

Dan Jacobs read off a bunch of facts that he considered most mundane. He gave Frank's date of birth, place of birth, education, grades, and grade point average in high school and college. He read the address of every place Frank had lived in his life.

"What were his parents' names and occupations?" Lucas asked. Dan read the names and gave the information. *Nothing special there,* he thought. But Lucas said, "Good, I thought so. I'm going to the beach for a couple of days. Call me if you need me."

"Lucas?" asked Dan. "What are we supposed to do? Everybody is asking questions, and you're leaving?"

"I'm not leaving. I've got some paperwork to catch up on. Just don't tell anybody anything. By the time I get back, it will all be over with, and you can go back to counting the days until you retire. Thanks, buddy."

"Sure, Lucas. No problem," said Dan, and as he hung up the phone, he was thinking what an asshole Lucas had turned out to be.

Lucas smiled. Now it made sense what had happened. Now he could solve the problem. He knew where they were going. He didn't know when they would get there or if they were already there, but he could find them now. It would all be over soon.

CHAPTER 17

Frank woke Morgan up in the hotel room, shaking her gently and offering her a cup of coffee. Had they met under different circumstances, he could have been a man very dear to her heart. Coffee in bed was a definite plus in her opinion.

"C'mon, dear. We've got to get going. The sun's going down, and we've got to get moving."

"What happened to me?" Morgan asked.

"Well, basically, shock and exhaustion, I imagine. You're tired and scared, your wrist is broken, and you haven't had too much sleep. You passed out. When you started to wake up, I gave you a pain pill, and you zonked out again. No big deal, but we've got to go now. Can you get up?"

"Where are we going?" Morgan asked.

"I'll tell you in the car. The sun's going down, and it'll make the car more difficult to spot, so none of Lucas's goons could spot us. I stole a car so they won't recognize us hopefully."

"Aren't you with the FBI?" Morgan asked.

"You know I am."

"Then can I ask why we're stealing a car? I mean, my god, I'm already wanted for murder, and now you want me to commit car theft?"

"Only as an accomplice. Seriously, we'll fix it later. No problem," he said and smiled.

"Why is it that you look like you're having fun?" Morgan asked, rather annoyed.

"Well, you have turned into quite the little challenge, and there's really nothing left to do but ride this out. It's kind of fun, really," he said and smiled.

"Fun? This is not my idea of fun!"

Frank just smiled and headed out the door. Then he turned and said, "You know, you'd probably have much better luck with men if you didn't wake up so grumpy."

Morgan tried to kick him, missed, and almost fell out the motel door. He just laughed, and that just made Morgan all the angrier. They walked out into the darkening parking lot. Morgan watched, dumbfounded, as Frank walked straight to a luxury sedan. Morgan assumed that it had been what he was so happy about. He seemed rather proud of himself. "You stole a car? I thought the whole idea was to be inconspicuous. You're insane," Morgan said.

"Could be, but everyone is thinking we would be trying to hide, right? So then why would we steal a car, a nice one at that, and drive straight up the highway? See, it's a marvelous plan," he said.

"Well, it's a plan anyway. How marvelous—that remains to be seen," she answered.

"Just get in the car, Morgan. We've got a long way to go tonight, and I want to get there before dawn."

"Where are we going?"

"Just get in the car, please."

Morgan didn't know it then, but they had been gone from the motel about ten minutes when the door to the motel room was kicked in and four of Atlanta's finest officers were tearing the room apart, looking for Frank and Morgan and any clue leading to them. Before they could leave, the manager of the motel came down to the room, yelling about all the commotion. As he walked through the doorway, one of the policemen simply shot him between the eyes and pulled his body fully into the room.

One of the men saw Morgan's half-empty cup of coffee on the table. "It's still warm," he said to the others as he picked up the cup. The four men left the room and calmly walked down to the office to look through the records to see how Frank had registered and what car tag number he had given. It took less than a minute for them to realize the car Frank had been driving, his own, was still parked behind the hotel.

"Maybe they just went to get dinner," said one.

"Well, if they did, Frank's not going to walk back in here with the door busted down," said the tall one.

"They still would have to come and get the car," said another.

"Maybe, but I doubt it," said the first one.

"You call it in, and we'll stay put for a few hours and see if they turn up. You and Joe go check the bus terminal and see if they skipped town that way. Hurry up."

For a moment, Dan Jacobs was relieved. He had called Lucas back with the information about Frank Haggarty, and Lucas, for once, had seemed satisfied. *Not that Lucas was ever satisfied with anything,* Dan thought. He briefly wondered why this one lady was so important to Lucas. After all, she did not have any prior arrests or convictions, and they all knew she hadn't killed the Henson fellow, so it was all just plain weird. Dan didn't spend too much time wondering about it though. Law enforcement was generally a strange job anyway, and soon Dan would be retiring—no more criminals, no more trials, and most importantly, no more Lucas Brown. A smile crossed Dan's face as he thought about that. Dan turned off his computer and began cleaning off his desk.

While the roads in Atlanta had pretty much been cleared of the snow, the yards were still covered with the crystallized water, and Dan found it to be quite lovely. *Maybe,* he thought, *my wife and I will have a late dinner in front of the fireplace and look out the windows onto the front yard and the snow.* As newlyweds, they had often spent evenings that way when they lived in Gatlinburg, Tennessee. Of course, that had been a lifetime ago—years before the birth of his daughter, a child so mentally handicapped that he and his wife had no choice but to institutionalize her, years before his lovely wife had suffered a nervous breakdown, years before he had transferred to Atlanta because the position paid more and he had been facing complete financial ruin with the expenses involved with caring for his daughter and later his wife.

The new position in Atlanta had helped, but Dan still had not been able to cover all his family's expenses.

Consequently, by the time Lucas had approached Dan with the proposition of providing a little extra inside information for a fee, Dan hadn't been able to refuse. Lucas, of course, knew precisely what Dan's situation was and precisely what Dan's response would be. Lucas never approached new contacts without knowing exactly how they would react. The two men had maintained the relationship for more than a decade.

Dan Jacobs was a man who loved his wife dearly. Their child's illness had been a strain on them both, but more so on his wife. She was so guilt-ridden that she could not accept the fact that her child would never improve and never have the mental maturity of a three-year-old and would probably die well before either Dan or her. Dan had watched helplessly as his wife visited one doctor after the other, specialist after specialist. Most of these visits provided no encouragement whatsoever, but all were incredibly expensive and not covered by insurance as the child's diagnosis had already been made. Insurance would not cover additional physician charges for the same diagnosis repeatedly.

After Dan had made his deal with Lucas, though, Dan was able to let his wife seek whatever medical opinions she wished for the child. Their daughter never improved, but his wife had found some sort of comfort, knowing she was doing everything humanly possible for her daughter. Even now, so many years later, his wife would still occasionally take the girl to another specialist, hoping against hope for some encouragement. Not once had Dan tried to stop his wife or complained about the expenses, and because of this, he was her hero. Indeed, that was what his wife thought every Sunday as they visited their daughter at the "home." His wife told him so, and that was all Dan really needed. Dan's wife had never questioned where Dan got the money for the doctors or how he was able to establish a trust account for his daughter that would provide for her for life, no matter how long she might live. It had taken him years, but he had done it.

Now finally, he was approaching retirement. He thanked God every morning that soon it would all end—no more favors for Lucas, no more illegal wiretaps, no more evidence to hide or to plant on a suspect, no more crime scenes to be tampered with, and no more bodies to hide. All this and more would soon end. As his daughter's financial needs were covered, Dan and his wife could comfortably live on his retirement. *Yes, thought Dan, I'll stop and buy my wife some roses on the way home.* He was smiling as he thought about the evening. It was sure to be a good evening. Dan Jacobs had never been so wrong about anything in his life.

CHAPTER 18

As Dan was thinking about the pleasant evening he was going to have, Frank and Morgan were driving north on Interstate 75; Lucas's hit squad was staked out at the motel, hoping for an opportunity to end the situation; Lucas was driving back to his office in Clarkston; and the FBI was scrambling to get agents to Lucas's office-condo at the beach and to the GBI office in Atlanta to grab Jacobs.

"How much longer do you think this will take?" Morgan asked as she stared at the lines on the highway.

"Why? Do you have somewhere to be?" was Frank's reply.

"Actually, yes. I need to be with my daughters."

"You need to tell me where they are so we can protect them, Morgan."

"Yeah, right. You guys have done a hell of a job protecting me."

"You're still alive, aren't you?"

Morgan looked out the car window and smoked a cigarette before she said anything else. "Why didn't you just take me back to your office?" she asked.

"Look, honey. If I took you back, you would've been dead by now. There wouldn't have been any way I could take care of you there. Too many people would've been able to reach you."

"Aren't you going to get in trouble for all of this? I mean, when it's all over, aren't you going to have a lot to answer to?"

"Yeah. I'm probably going to be fired, if I'm not already. I've broken more bureau regulations than I could ever get away with, and by the time we get where we're going, I could be charged with kidnapping you."

"Where are we going?"

"To a cabin up in the North Georgia Mountains. It's very secluded, and with the snow, it would just about be impossible to reach without snow chains on a car. If anyone comes close with chains on their tires, we're going to hear them. At least we won't be caught off guard."

"Then what happens? I mean, how do we get out of this?" Morgan asked. What she really wanted, or rather needed, was to be told everything was going to be fine. It would all work out, and everyone would live happily ever after.

"I don't know yet" was all Frank said. It wasn't quite the answer Morgan had hoped for.

It was quite dark as Lucas pulled into the parking lot of InterSecure Security. Now that he had figured out pretty much what had happened, he was certain he wouldn't be able to return to his old life and business, so he needed to grab some files and other items from the safe in his office. Two minutes, in and out, and he would be gone from Clarkston, Georgia, forever. Lucas sat in his car briefly and thought about Robert. He was probably the only truly honest man Lucas had ever known. Lucas thought briefly that he might actually miss Robert, but he knew he would never be able to give Robert an acceptable explanation as to what had happened. Some people, Lucas knew, simply let too much integrity rule their lives. Robert was one of those people, and Lucas really was not.

As Lucas entered the back door to his office building, he looked cautiously around to make sure no one was close enough to see him. The only light in the building came from the streetlights, casting strange shadows on the walls and floors inside the office. Lucas, satisfied that no one was near, walked down the hall and opened his office door. He was startled as he saw Robert sitting in the chair behind his desk. "Jesus, Robert! What the hell are you doing here in the dark?" asked Lucas.

"Lucas, we've got to have a serious talk. You need to tell me what's been going on."

"Sure, buddy. We'll sit down and talk it all out as soon as I get back. I'm going down to the condo for a couple of days, and as soon as I get back, I'll tell you everything."

"How about if I go with you? We'll have plenty of time to talk on the drive down."

"Sure, Robert, if that's what you want to do. Let me grab a couple of things, and we'll go."

Robert stood up from the chair and walked over to the window as Lucas sat behind his desk and collected folders. He placed the folders in his briefcase. When he was finished, he stood up and told Robert he was ready to go. The two men walked out of Lucas's office, but just as they cleared the doorway, Lucas stopped. "Damn, I forgot one folder. Hold on. I'll be right back," Lucas said. As he turned to head back to his office, Robert stopped in the hallway to wait. Before Robert was completely still, Lucas had gotten behind Robert and hit him on the side of his head with his revolver. Robert collapsed on the floor, blood streaming from his head, and Lucas went back to his office to clear out his safe. Thirty seconds later, Lucas stepped over his unconscious business partner and friend and left the building.

Frank was humming along to the radio as he drove north on the interstate.

"Why are you so happy?" asked Morgan.

"Not particularly happy, just thinking" was the reply.

"Where are we going, Frank?"

"To a cabin, right by the state line," Frank answered.

"You rented a cabin?"

"No, it used to be my dad's. I inherited it after he died."

"You mean after Lucas killed him?" Morgan said and was immediately sorry she had opened her mouth.

Frank slammed on the brakes and nearly crashed into the guardrail, trying to pull over to the shoulder of the highway. He was trying to regain his composure, but he yelled at Morgan anyway, "How in God's name do you know anything about my father?"

Morgan looked at Frank, who was glaring at her. His hands were wrapped tightly around the steering wheel, and he was fidgeting in his seat. But he never took his eyes off her. Morgan realized that whatever she said was critical because if Frank got seriously irritated with her, she'd be on her own and her chances of living long that way were about as good as an ice cube's chances in hell. "Look, Frank," she began, almost in a whisper, "John told me a few months ago that Lucas had killed your father. I really never would've even remembered, except when he told me about your dad. He had mentioned that your father had a son, you, who was in the FBI. I remember thinking you guys must have had law enforcement careers like the New York City firefighters do—you know, generation after generation. Kind of a family tradition thing.

"Anyway, by the time this whole thing turned into such a freaking mess, I figured the only way I had any kind of a chance was to find someone who had a reason to maybe listen to me, and you sprang to mind. A newspaper reporter couldn't help because I really can't prove anything. Any law enforcement agency would have just turned me over to one of Lucas's friends, so you were really my only shot. I'm sorry. I guess I should have said something before. I just didn't think it really mattered that I knew about your dad. I just thought it would maybe be the reason you might listen to me."

Frank took a deep breath, several actually, and tried to focus. His wife hadn't even known about Lucas. Hell, Frank would not have even known about Lucas, except his father had mailed him a letter a day before he had died. There really hadn't been many details in the letter, only a brief description of Lucas's liaison with Frank's father and his suspicions that Lucas was involved in many illegal activities. His dad had written he was concerned for his safety but was honor bound to do his duty.

Naturally, at the crime scene, there had been no evidence. There was only the body of Frank's father, his throat sliced open from ear to ear. Frank had never told anyone of the letter because he could not prove anything. He had spent the last two years of his life trying to figure out what he was missing in the letter, what clue his father had left him that he could not find. *Maybe though,* thought Frank, *the letter hadn't been intended to be a clue. Maybe my dad was warning me to stay away from Lucas.* Frank had never thought of that as an option, and he really did not have time at the moment. He'd think about it later, when all this was over. Right now, there was way too much to do.

Frank pulled slowly back onto the interstate. Morgan was most relieved that he had not simply thrown her out on the side of the road. "Any more secrets, Morgan?"

"Nope, no more."

"Then we're going to start all over again, and you're going to tell me every word of every conversation you ever had with John."

"Frank, honest to God, I've told you everything I can think of. I just didn't tell you about your dad 'cause I didn't want to get you upset."

"Start talking, Morgan. Word for word."

As Lucas pulled out of the parking lot of his office building, he was having second thoughts. He was not sure if he should have killed Robert or if he had killed Robert. He thought about going back to see what exactly the situation was, but that would be far too risky. Robert might have regained consciousness by now, and then Lucas would have to kill him. If Robert was already dead, going back would not possibly do any good. If Robert was alive, it was a certainty that Lucas Brown would never go back to his office at InterSecure Security ever again. The deeper this mess got, the more certain Lucas was that his life in Clarkston was over. He wondered where his new life would begin. He wondered what his new assignment would entail. Lucas had never really minded changes, and he loved a good challenge, so he was not particularly worried about the next phase of his career.

Actually, Lucas thought things were progressing rather well, with the exception of Robert. He knew where Frank and Morgan were, and it would simply be a matter of getting rid of them—no witnesses, no hassles. He just had to find out from Morgan how much she knew and where her kids were. They, too, had to be eliminated just to keep things clean. His bosses in Washington were not very pleased, but once he has a chance to explain, Lucas was certain they would agree with his choice of action. No one could have predicted this would happen. *All in all,* thought Lucas, *this just might work out for the best.*

Frank continued to drill Morgan with questions until she thought she would lose her mind. She understood that he thought she was holding out on him, but the truth was, she had never really known what this was about and assumed she never would. "Jesus, Frank. Will you please shut up!" Morgan shouted.

"Morgan, you've got to talk to me."

"Well, how about this? I don't know what to tell you because I don't know what the hell this is about. I miss my kids, and I want to go see them. How in the hell are you going to fix this?"

"I don't know. Lucas knows where we're going. I'm certain of that. So by the time he gets there, we've either got to be able to nail him or we've got a bigger problem than we do now."

"Why in God's name are we going somewhere that Lucas knows to look for us?" Morgan screamed.

"Because it gives us the home-court advantage. I know the land. Lucas doesn't. And if we can figure out what you know that you don't think you know, we can have him picked up. If not, we'll just have to fight it out."

"You're crazy! I'm not going anywhere I know Lucas is going to show up. Just drop me off in the next town. I'll take my own chances. Jesus Christ, you're as crazy as he is. I don't need this. Just let me out!"

"I'm all you've got, sweetheart, so just calm down. I'm not going to let Lucas hurt you. I promise."

"And just how do you think you're going to keep that from happening?"

"I don't know really. I'm still working on a plan."

"Gee, Frank, I feel so much better."

Frank laughed and kept on driving. Morgan curled up in the seat and pretended to try to sleep.

CHAPTER 19

Robert was still lying unconscious on the hallway floor when the FBI arrived. They immediately called an ambulance, but Robert was awake by the time the paramedics arrived. An FBI agent asked Robert to accompany him to a local hotel where the FBI had set up their headquarters, and Robert readily agreed. The paramedics bandaged his head, and Robert left with the agent. He was more than a little curious about what was happening, and he assumed he could at least fill them in on his earlier conversation with Jim. Robert no longer felt any loyalty to his former business partner and friend.

Dan Jacobs had just shut the door to his office and was heading home to his wife as he saw the five men walking down the hall. He instinctively knew there was a problem, and he felt his stomach immediately tie up in knots. "How can I help you, gentlemen?" Dan asked, trying to appear pleasant.

"Daniel Jacobs?" the man in front asked.

"Yes."

"FBI," the man said and showed his identification. "We need to speak to you regarding the activities of a Lucas Brown. I assume you know the person in question?"

"Only professionally. How can I help you?"

"Can we go in your office, sir? This might take a while."

"Sure." Dan knew this. Dan had almost made it, almost retired. All he needed to do was work out the rest of his time, but Lucas just couldn't let this thing go. Dan felt like crying but knew he could not allow himself to do so. They descended upon him like locusts. As soon as Dan had opened the door to his office, all five of the agents had begun firing questions at him. Dan was used to this and had participated in many similar questionings but always as the one asking, never the one expected to answer. He answered the initial round of questions as vaguely as possible while still giving the appearance of cooperating. He tried to appear calm, but despite himself, he had broken into a sweat.

The FBI agents knew they had him; it was simply a matter of how long it took for him to crack. Dan asked if he could take a break and call his wife to tell her he'd be late coming home. The agents readily agreed but not before they suggested he might not be going home for several days. Dan pretended to ignore the comment and called his wife.

Frank's boss, Harry Sprewell, was waiting at the hotel for his men to bring in Robert. A scenario had unfolded in front of them. And while everyone now knew Lucas Brown had probably killed John Henson, definitely assaulted Robert and Jim, requested numerous illegal wiretaps, and in all likelihood, was out to kill this girl named Morgan, they still had no idea why. Background checks on Lucas had revealed nothing but an exemplary record of both military and civil service. However, the agency had had difficulty even running the check as his records had initially been classified. It had taken several calls to the justice department in Washington to get his information released. There had also been a brief phone call from a desk jockey, with the CIA asking questions. This was beyond bad.

Harry Sprewell could sense they were on to something incredibly big, but he had no idea what it was or how he was going to find out. Furthermore, he had not heard from Frank since the day before and was not even certain his agent was still alive. Sprewell was most interested in talking to Robert to learn what he might know.

Morgan had been looking out of the car window for the last hour. It was pitch-black outside, with nothing to see except the lines on the road and the snow piled up on the highway's shoulder. "Frank?"

"Yeah?"

"How do you think this is going to end?"

"I don't know, Morgan. I wish I did."

"Isn't there somebody you can call and just get this fixed?"

"I still don't know what I'm trying to fix, Morgan. All I know is that you say you saw somebody get killed on your porch and that you were with me while you were supposedly killing your lover, John. You've got to tell me what it is Lucas needs from you."

"I don't know anything," Morgan said and sighed. She sounded tired, and Frank felt somewhat sorry for her.

"I think you know something that John told you, but when he did, you thought it was so insignificant that you haven't remembered yet. If you really don't know anything, Lucas certainly thinks you do." Frank glanced over at Morgan as he drove. For the first time, he really saw her for what she really was—a scared young woman who had fallen in love with the wrong guy. Nothing more, nothing less.

There was something different about her though. As scared as she was, she had the sense to think. She had found Frank because she realized she needed someone with a personal interest in what she was saying, and she had been wise enough to hide her kids. Frank smiled. The kid had guts, and he liked that. "What are you going to do when this is over?" he asked her.

"I have no idea."

"Do you have any money stashed away?"

"Nope, not a dime. Everything is gone."

"Any family you and your kids can stay with for a while?"

"Not really. My folks are dead. I've got a few cousins, but nobody really close. I'm sure no one is going to be real excited about talking to me since everyone I knew got hauled in to the police station. I'm sure that does wonders for friendships."

"You never know, hon. I'm sure someone will help. Most people are inherently good."

"You know, Frank, this is the first time in my life I don't know what I'm going to do. Honestly, I haven't got a clue." Morgan felt a hopeless feeling creeping into her chest and could feel her eyes begin to tear, so she decided to change the subject. "What are you going to do, Frank? When all of this is over?"

Frank looked surprised and asked her what she meant.

"I think you should find your wife and make up with her."

"What makes you think she'd have anything to do with me now?"

"Well, when you talk about her, your eyes are full of love. And I bet since you love her so much, if you told her everything, gave her an honest explanation, she'd take you back."

Frank smiled. "You know, you sort of remind me of her when she was younger. All spunk and vigor, never to be defeated."

"So just go back and win her over again."

"My dad had a saying, Morgan. He used to say, 'That's why men chase women and women conquer.' I could chase this woman for the rest of my life and might not ever catch her. On the other hand, she conquered me years ago. I'd never love anyone else."

Morgan smiled then. She thought what Frank was saying was sweet. She also thought even though several men had chased her in her young life, she did not feel that she had ever conquered any of them—all in one's perception of things, she supposed.

CHAPTER 20

Robert gladly left the InterSecure office and rode in silence as the agent drove the short distance to the hotel where the FBI had temporarily stationed themselves. His head was pounding—understandably so as the paramedics had cautioned he had a moderately severe concussion and really needed to be kept in the hospital for observation. Robert, however, could not have cared less about his health at the moment. He was furious at Lucas. Robert's reputation was at stake, the business was ruined, and he had no clue why. Furthermore, Lucas had assaulted both him and Jim and apparently was after Morgan as well. Robert could not see any connection between the events, but he was certain there had to be one. Robert sighed. He was certain it was going to be a very long night.

Once the five agents in Dan's office had presented him with copies of his financial records, including details of his daughter's trust fund, Dan knew everything was all over for him. He did not need the agents to explain what was going to happen next. He would be arrested. All his assets, his daughter's trust fund included, would be frozen as evidence. Dan would lose his retirement and his pension. Next would come the humiliation of the trial and subsequent conviction, with Dan living out his remaining years in prison alongside inmates he had helped put there.

Dan was not worried so much about what his peers and friends would think, but he did care about his wife. She would be devastated. Furthermore, once she realized their daughter would be sent to a state-run facility because they would not have any money, she would be inconsolable. His wife had never been able to accept less than the very best of care for their daughter, and given the current state of things, Dan was not going to be in a position to pay for any care at all. No, his wife was not going to be able to accept this at all.

Dan was almost relieved, though. For more than thirty years, he had taken care of everything. Mentally, he was tired. Certainly, his life was ruined, as well as his wife's and daughter's. But maybe, just maybe, he could correct some serious injustices. The five agents in Dan's office listened in stunned silence as Dan described, in detail, accounts of false imprisonment, forged court orders, illegal search warrants, illegal wiretaps, witness tampering, and more. Three hours passed with only Dan talking. The agents did not dare interrupt as they did not want him to clam up.

When Dan finally paused for a moment, he asked one of the agents if he could get a folder from a file cabinet. The agent nodded, and Dan got up and retrieved a thick folder. The contents of the folder read as a novel. There were dates, names, times, and actions taken all on Lucas Brown's behalf. It was a most damning set of documents as all the information was verifiable. Dan almost laughed as he handed the file folder to the agents. Lucas would have killed him on the spot had he known such a folder even existed. At least, in the end, Dan would somewhat be able to even the score.

"Can I go to the restroom?" asked Dan.

"Sure," said one of the men and told two others to accompany Dan down the hallway.

The three agents remaining in Dan's office stared at one another in disbelief. "What in the hell have we stumbled on here?"

"God, it'll take years to sort through this stuff. Can you imagine all of the overturned convictions if this goes public? The state of Georgia would go bankrupt with all of the lawsuits bound to follow."

"I'm calling Harry," said the third.

"Tell them to arrest him when he comes out of the restroom. I don't care what you charge him with. We'll just add to it as we go. He'll never be granted bail anyway, so he's not going anywhere."

All three men nodded in agreement. None of them knew exactly what to say.

It had not taken too long for Daniel Jacobs to break down. As soon as the agents played back the tapes of Dan giving Lucas Frank's home address and then the background information on Frank, Dan knew it was basically over. They had him dead to rights. His only hope now was to be allowed to resign and take an early retirement. Of course, he knew that wasn't going to happen either.

Standing in the men's restroom of the fourth floor of the Georgia Bureau of Investigations, Dan realized he was at the end. He found small consolation, hoping the evidence in the folder would lead to Lucas's downfall. Dan wasn't even very hopeful of that, for Lucas had connections, a lot of connections. And no matter what Lucas did, he always seemed to land on his feet. Dan, looking in the mirror, couldn't say he recognized the man in the mirror. All he had ever wanted to do was to provide for his family and be a loving and supportive husband and father. Somewhere, it had gotten all screwed up. It just didn't seem fair.

Taking a paper towel from the dispenser on the wall, Dan wrote "Tell my wife I love her" on the towel, folded it, and placed it neatly on the counter by the sink. Calmly he drew his service revolver and placed the gun in his mouth. His hand trembled, and a single tear ran down his face. He was staring in the mirror as he pulled the trigger, blowing the back of his skull off. Daniel Jacobs would never again do any favors for Lucas Brown.

Harry Sprewell was on the phone, listening dumbfounded to the agent in Atlanta who held Dan's secret folder in his hands.

"Harry," said the agent, "if a third of this is true, you could arrest and convict half of the law enforcement officials in Georgia and a bunch of elected ones right along with them."

Robert walked in the hotel room at this moment. Harry glanced up long enough to see who had entered and motioned for Robert to take a seat. Returning to the phone call, Harry said, "Fax over what you have and get Jacobs down here." He hung up the phone. Turning to look at

Robert, Harry said, "Mr. Smith, I certainly hope you can shed some light on this situation for me."

Robert smiled and replied, "I was hoping you could do the same for me."

Roughly two seconds passed between the time Dan pulled the trigger and the time the two agents who had accompanied him down the hall raced into the restroom.

"Oh," said the first one.

"Son of a gun," said the second as he surveyed the scene. "I'll call Harry."

Harry did not need to go to the scene to look. Another phone call was made, and quickly, the GBI building was flooded with FBI agents and technicians. Computers were confiscated, and file cabinets were sealed and removed from the building. Anyone who had worked with Dan over the last ten years was immediately sought for questioning. Agents were dispatched to search Dan's home and to question both his wife and daughter.

Understandably, the director of the Georgia Bureau of Investigations was most upset. He had not been informed of anything until Dan's suicide. He honestly had not a clue what had transpired in his offices, but his career was sure to end in very short order. The director would find very little comfort later, realizing dozens of careers were going to end right along with his.

Harry Sprewell was furious that his agents had been careless enough to allow Daniel Jacobs to commit suicide. Technically, they were extending a professional courtesy, particularly since he had been so cooperative, but they should have realized how emotionally distraught he would have been. They had committed an unnecessary, careless mistake, and now a potential witness was lost.

Harry and Robert quickly formed a working relationship. Harry believed Robert had no idea what Lucas was doing but also believed Robert could provide some useful information on Lucas's associates, habits, and personality traits. Robert had immediately suggested they call Jim Jackson and that Harry speak to Jim about his relationship with

Lucas. Jim was on his way to the hotel while Harry and Robert tried to determine what should be done next.

Technicians were picking apart the computer terminals at the InterSecure office but, so far, had not come up with anything unusual.

"I just don't see a connection between your guy Frank and Morgan and Lucas. It just doesn't make any sense," said Robert to Harry.

"I don't know. Frank refused to bring her in after the warrant was issued for her for the Henson murder. Frank thought he was on to something, but after his house was ransacked, he went on the run with her. He said we couldn't keep her safe. The way this is looking, he was probably right."

"I know Morgan though. She's a fantastic businesswoman, made some mistakes about men, but definitely not a criminal at all."

"Are you sure, Robert? Couldn't she have been doing something illegal with John or Lucas?"

"No way. She loves her kids too much."

"Even good people make bad mistakes when they need money."

"Not her, no way."

Harry shrugged. He hadn't heard from Frank since he had called from the little motel, the same motel that now had the dead night manager. Harry was fairly certain Frank was still alive, though, or Lucas would not have been in such a hurry to get away from Robert. Even though no one seriously thought Lucas would show up at the beachfront condo, agents were already there, staking out the location just in case. Harry barked out more commands. There were more things to look for, and agents and technicians scrambled from the hotel room to fulfill their assigned tasks.

CHAPTER 21

Just as they reached the Georgia–North Carolina state line, Frank pulled into a small convenience store. He left the car running, heater on, and told Morgan to stay put. He returned a few minutes later with bacon, eggs, milk, and a carton of cigarettes. "Everything else we need is already there," Frank said as he climbed back into the car.

"Any rum and coke there?"

"Certainly is."

"Coffee?"

"Yes, ma'am. Everything you need to be happy." Frank was grinning as he pulled out of the parking lot.

Morgan momentarily entertained the idea of her and Frank as a couple. She couldn't imagine why his wife would have left him. Under different circumstances, Morgan would find herself most attracted to this man. She wondered if this was the real Frank or just the professional side of him showing. She decided it really didn't matter one way or the other. He was all she had right now, and she was certainly hoping this was all part of God's plan for them.

Lucas was deep in thought as he drove north on the interstate. He would have preferred to have a little more preparation time, a more solid plan, but he had been trained for such eventualities and was certain he would have a better course of action planned once he arrived at his destination. Lucas remembered the cabin well. He had even spent a night there once with Frank's father, the two men fishing and drinking as if they were actually friends.

Lucas had misjudged Frank's father, though. Lucas had dropped hints to the man for months to see how he would react to certain things. As he had never questioned him, Lucas decided Frank's father might fit in well. Lucas tried to bring him into the loop, tried to make him part of an elite group of trusted individuals. After all, the pay was fantastic, and he would be serving his country on one of the highest levels imaginable.

Initially, the conversation had gone quite well. Frank's father had seemed genuinely interested in participating, but when Lucas touched on the Kennedy thing and the continued maintenance of the situation, the man had balked. Frank's father had even threatened to expose Lucas and his organization. A seasoned FBI agent, he had shocked Lucas by declaring that the American public had a right to know about such things. Lucas knew this was inaccurate. Not only did the American public really not have a right to know, they didn't really want to know. The average American would never even be able to understand the truth, much less form a legitimate opinion on whether certain activities were justified or not. Sometimes, people had to die. Some people had to make great sacrifices whether they chose to or not. It was just the way of things.

Once Frank's father had mentioned going to the press with what Lucas had told him, there had been no other options. Lucas had started laughing, said he was just joking around and none of it was true. Eventually, Frank's father had gotten up to fix another drink. As he did so, Lucas stepped behind him, grabbed his forehead, and pulling his head back, slit the man's throat cleanly from ear to ear. The elder Haggarty had not even had a chance to utter a word. Lucas liked it that way. He didn't have anything else to say anyway.

Two years had passed since then. No one had known the men were meeting at the cabin, and naturally, Lucas didn't leave behind any evidence. The murder had never been solved. *Actually,* mused Lucas, *it had been one of my easier kills.* Lucas had been calm enough to go into the kitchen and fix a turkey and cheese sandwich. Mindful of his health, he had poured a glass of milk to go with the meal and ate his lunch, sitting at the kitchen table where he had an unobstructed view of the lifeless body in the living room. Having finished his lunch, Lucas meticulously wiped his fingerprints from everything in the cabin and gone on his way. He had been smiling as he left. It was just all so easy.

Once again concentrating on the highway, Lucas hoped Frank would be as easy as his father had been to kill. Surely with Frank out of the way, Morgan would quickly tell Lucas what he needed to know. It would only be a matter of time. Lucas grew excited just thinking about it. The thought of killing Morgan was most appealing. Hell, he might even rape her before it was over. John had taken her, so Lucas didn't see why he shouldn't. He and John had been the closest of friends after all. The only question remaining for Lucas was how he would kill her. Would he do it fast and merciful or slow and painful? She had caused him a great deal of inconvenience. He would think more about it, but he was definitely leaning toward a slow, painful death for Morgan.

Robert, Harry, and Jim quickly went over Jim's story of basic blackmail by Lucas and the subsequent beating Jim had received by Lucas's own hands. The faxed copies of Dan's folder came in, and the three men read in disbelief the numerous accounts of illegal activities. All three agreed that Lucas must have been receiving payment from someone for these services, but no one knew from whom. They just couldn't connect the clues; there didn't seem to be a common link.

"Maybe we're looking the wrong way," said Harry. "Could it be a lover's quarrel?"

"No way," said Robert.

"She was so hung up on John she wouldn't even look at anyone else," said Jim.

"Anyway, wouldn't have your agent just brought her in for questioning if it were that simple? Not to mention, Lucas, or someone, has totally destroyed this man's house. That's a bit more than an act of jealousy, if you ask me," said Robert.

As the three men again grew quiet, mulling over the situation, an agent walked in with background information, business associates, family members' names and addresses, occupations of them all, and every other known fact about Frank, Lucas, and Morgan. It was a rather ominous pile of paper.

"Harry," said Robert, "I'd be glad to take a copy of this and go over it at home. My head's pounding, and I really need to go home and get some rest. I'll be back first thing in the morning, if that's all right with you."

"Sure," said Harry, and he directed another agent to give Robert a similar stack of papers and bid them good night.

"C'mon," said Jim. "I'll drive you home."

"Thanks."

Once in his car and pulling away from the hotel, Jim asked, "OK, where are we going?"

"Somewhere we can get coffee and figure this out. It's too noisy in there."

Jim smiled even though his ribs ached. He had known all along Robert had no intention of returning home until this was over. Robert wanted to find Lucas first.

Harry was once again barking out orders. He was on the phone, telling yet another agent to find a judge willing to sign an arrest warrant in the middle of the night for Lucas Brown. He also wanted photos of Morgan, Frank, and Lucas faxed to every police department in the country. Harry was tired of waiting. He wanted them found.

"Yes, sir" were the only words spoken on the other end of the phone line.

Snow began to fall again as Frank pulled up to the base of a long, steep driveway. A wooden cabin sat at the top of the incline, nestled among the trees, and was silhouetted only by the moonlight.

"This is it," said Frank. "Were going to have to walk up the drive, though. The driveway is frozen, and this caddy isn't going to make the climb."

"Where are we?" asked Morgan.

"The great Appalachian Mountains of North Carolina. C'mon, let's get climbing."

The two got out of the car, with Frank carrying the bags of groceries, and began to slowly work their way up the driveway. Morgan, who had not been out of the car and away from the heater for hours, was immediately struck by how cold it was. She looked around at the falling snowflakes and thought how much her daughters would have loved to be able to be playing in the snow. She could just picture them running around, screaming in joy, trying to catch the falling flakes, and building snowmen. The thought made her heart ache. She missed them.

Finally, they reached the top of the drive and slid their way up the stairs to the porch to the front door of the cabin. Frank tentatively opened the front door to the cabin and looked inside. Frank had not come back to this place since the day he had found his father's body. Morgan, of course, had no way of knowing this and was anxious to get inside and warm up. She more or less pushed Frank through the front door. Frank shot Morgan a look of disapproval but continued to go in anyway.

The temperature inside was exactly the same as the temperature outside as there had not been any heat in the cabin. This disappointed Morgan greatly.

"Have a seat on the sofa, Morgan. It'll just take me a minute to get a fire going. It'll warm you up in no time."

"Sure, whatever you say." Morgan sat on the sofa and looked around the cabin while she waited for Frank to return. The living room appeared to be cozy. Quilts draped the back of the sofa and reclining chair. A small oak desk was positioned against one wall. The fireplace consumed the wall opposite the sofa. A doorway led to the kitchen, which Morgan could also see from her position on the couch. The mantle above the fireplace was filled with family photographs. One picture was of several people, presumably Frank's parents, his wife, and children. Another picture was just Frank and a man who had to be his father. The resemblance of one to the other was undeniable. Several other photographs were the children by themselves doing various things, such as fishing, skiing, and playing in the snow. Morgan thought they certainly looked happy, just like the perfect American family.

Looking at the photographs made Morgan think of her own family, and she was struck with an overwhelming sadness of how much she missed her own parents. They had been dead for years, but suddenly, it felt as if she had just heard the news of their deaths. She felt incredibly lost. She had nowhere to go and nowhere to be. She could not imagine feeling more lost and alone than she did at this moment.

Frank came back in the room with an armful of small logs and kindling for the fire. He stacked the log perfectly, placed the kindling underneath, and struck a match. A small piece of the kindling immediately caught on fire, and the flames rapidly began spreading from one piece of kindling to the next. Moments later, a modest fire was producing heat, and the cabin began to warm.

"That's pretty impressive," said Morgan, commenting on how quickly Frank had been able to get the fire going.

"I was a Boy Scout." Frank smiled.

"I'm sure you were."

"I'll go make some coffee. Then we'll talk some more."

Frank disappeared through the doorway to the kitchen. Morgan could hear utensils clanging around in the kitchen and tried to keep from laughing. Frank may have had the perfect family, but his wife had obviously done all the cooking. Morgan stood up and stretched and walked over to the fireplace. She poked at the logs and watched the flames.

Eventually, Frank emerged with two steaming cups of coffee. "Here, hon. This should warm you up," he said. "Are you hungry?"

"Not really," she replied.

"OK, have you remembered anything else?"

"No," said Morgan, sitting on the sofa again.

Frank sat down next to her. Neither one of them said anything for about five minutes. Finally, Frank began to talk. "The last time I came here, I found my father."

"Was he lost?"

"I found my father's body here. I haven't been here since."

Morgan could have kicked herself for being such an idiot. Hopefully, Frank would realize she had not meant the comment the way it had sounded. "I'm sorry" was all she could think to say.

"I pay a guy down the road to check on the place, you know, kind of keep it up. But I never planned on coming here again."

"Then why did we come here, Frank?"

"Because, eventually, Lucas will figure out we're here."

"And this is your idea of a good thing?"

"Well, maybe."

"Well, maybe not!" Morgan was furious again. "I would say if Lucas is certain to come here, then here is the last place on earth I would choose to be!"

"Here we can see him coming, Morgan. He'll have to come in through the front door, so he will lose the element of surprise. If he drives up, we'll hear him because there's never any traffic. And if he walks up, we'll see him. I'll keep you safe. I promise."

"Like I have a choice. This is just wonderful."

Frank looked at her. She reminded him of a young schoolgirl. Her hair was tangled, and her clothes wrinkled. The sweatshirt she was wearing was about five sizes too large, and the sleeves covered her hands. Sitting on the sofa at that moment, she looked like she was pouting. Frank reached out and gently pulled her head over to his shoulder. She let him, and he gently stroked her hair, hoping somehow she would feel reassured. She never said anything and seemed to fall asleep in a matter of minutes.

Frank remained on the sofa, stroking her hair and looking at the flames in the fireplace. He tried to tell himself he was only doing his job. He could not have taken her into custody because Lucas, with all his clout, would have had access to Morgan and she would be dead. He did want to keep her safe. He believed Morgan about really not knowing anything. He also wanted to face Lucas. He wanted to hear Lucas say he had murdered his father. Frank wanted to kill him. Momentarily, Frank wondered if he might be using Morgan to have a chance to kill Lucas or if he was really trying to do his job. He had way too many things to think about, though, to ponder about that at the time.

CHAPTER 22

Word of Dan Jacob's suicide had spread quickly among the Georgia Bureau of Investigation employees. News of a warrant for the arrest of Lucas Brown might as well had been broadcast on the national news. Phones were ringing off the hooks between police officers, judges, attorneys, private investigators, and bail bondsmen. Most were shocked, some were worried, and some were just plain elated. As the faxes were being broadcast across the country, Lucas received a page on his beeper. It was a five-digit number, but if one matched the numbers to the letters on a telephone keypad and then unscrambled the letters, one would have come up with a-b-o-r-t. Lucas did not have to unscramble the letters. He knew the codes. Lucas also knew the rules. Given an abort message, he was to immediately cease his activities and go into hiding until he was contacted. He was not to contact anyone. He was not to do anything further.

Lucas pulled over to the side of the highway. He was momentarily confused. Never had he been given an order to stop. He had never left an assignment unfinished. There must be a mistake. The consequences of not finishing this would be incomprehensible. There was far too much at stake for any of them to stop now. Lucas would call. Surely someone had made an erroneous decision. Lucas dialed a number on his cell phone. As the call was answered, Lucas said, "2-1-9-7-2-3."

There was no response on the other end, but a series of clicking sounds signaled the call was being transferred.

"Why did you call here?" was the greeting from an angry voice.

"I believe there has been a mistake," said Lucas.

"You have made the mistake. We cannot and will not protect you now. You are on your own. Disappear and do not contact us again." The line went silent.

The man on the other end of the phone line pushed an intercom button on his desk. "Get someone down to Georgia. Brown needs to be eliminated immediately." There was no reply, but the anonymous man knew his instructions had been heard.

Lucas's brain could not accept the prior conversation. It was beyond his comprehension that he would ever hear the words just spoken to him. He was so close! He almost had her, and the whole mess would be cleaned up—no Morgan, no loose ends. He could not quit now. It was impossible. He was more certain than ever that they had simply made a mistake.

His first move was to call Dan. Lucas tried the office first. No answer. He tried Dan's home number. Again, no answer. Lucas dialed Dan's cell phone and was immediately connected to voice mail. Frustrated, Lucas pounded the dashboard of his car. He would kick Dan's butt when he would return to Atlanta. Dan knew to always be available for Lucas. Next, Lucas tried two other contacts he knew in the GBI. Again, there was no response.

Finally, on his sixth try, Lucas was able to connect with one of his contacts. "What in the hell is going on?" Lucas screamed into the phone.

"Man, you are in this deep! Dan blew his brains out, and the FBI is all over the place. They have an arrest warrant for you. You need to leave. Just go."

"They have a warrant for what?" Lucas asked.

"Pretty much anything you can think of, man" was the reply.

Robert and Jim had been sitting in the back-corner booth of the local coffee shop. Papers were spread all over the booth, and Robert was wildly jotting down notes.

"Robert, what do you think you're looking for?" Jim asked.

"Anything. There's got to be a link between John and Frank somehow."

"How do you know that?"

"Because, presumably, Morgan did not know Frank until she called him. But she called and specifically asked for Frank, so John had to have said to Morgan something about Frank. Maybe John had said nothing more than Frank was a good cop. Who knows?"

"And Lucas and John were close friends for years, and now suddenly, John is dead. I'm sure by Lucas's hands. And Lucas thinks Morgan knows something John knew," Jim stated.

"Exactly," said Robert. "Lucas is scared of something she knows. Keep looking. Frank and Morgan can't have much time left before Lucas catches up with them."

"Do you think we can find them first?" asked Jim.

"I'd be happy to get there before Morgan gets killed," Robert replied.

"What do you think will happen to Lucas?"

"I don't know," said Robert. "But I do know he's got a lot of questions to answer."

The two men continued sifting through the mound of papers, frustrated at not being able to find a clue.

All Lucas needed to do was to leave the country. The glove compartment of his car contained three different sets of passports, driver's licenses, and credit cards. Lucas could become any of these fake people with ease. One was a teacher, one a stockbroker, and one a businessman. No one alive knew Lucas had these items, not even his former employer, so Lucas would be able to disappear completely. All he needed to do was to drive to the nearest airport and catch the first plane out the country.

A duffel bag in the trunk of his car contained enough money for Lucas to live on for the rest of his life—maybe not enough to live lavishly but definitely enough to be comfortable. Lucas could, if he chose, go back to work with a real job. He could make a few investments and possibly even remarry without having to go through the hassle of getting divorced first. Most men would have been grateful for such a simple solution for such a complex problem. Lucas could not even consider this scenario as an option. He simply could not do so. He had spent his entire adult life serving his country. Occasionally, yes, he had been paid on the side to do certain jobs. But his main concern had always been to keep tabs on his men. Those stupid old men like John, unfortunately, seemed to be ridden with guilty consciences as they grew older.

Until recently, months and sometimes years had passed without Lucas needing to do anything. Then someone would get drunk and start running off at the mouth, and Lucas would have to go to work. Usually, a warning would be sufficient. But when that wasn't sufficient to stop the issue, Lucas would quickly end the problem by ending a life; sometimes, several lives.

Lucas could not fathom being considered a criminal. He had been legally committing murder for years. It really wasn't legal at all, but the government allowed him to do so. And that was all the approval Lucas needed. The very idea that someone might question him infuriated Lucas.

No, thought Lucas, *I'm not ready for this to end yet. And if it does, it certainly isn't going to be because of Morgan.* Lucas would simply continue on with his plan, and after Morgan told him all she knew, he would dispose of her. After that, Lucas would find her children, and to be on the safe side, he would kill them too—no loose ends, no incriminations. Upon completing his mission, Lucas would make his way back to Washington and explain the situation. He was certain he could make them see their error. Once the problem was eliminated, he was sure they would need him again. Lucas's reputation would be restored again. He was certain of this.

"I've got it!" shouted Robert.

"What'd you find?" asked Jim.

"Frank Haggarty Sr., I assume Frank's dad, worked on a case in Williamstown in '98. John was chief of police then."

"OK, so where do we find Frank Sr. and have a talk with him?"

"This says he was murdered a couple of years ago at a family cabin in North Carolina."

"Robbery?"

"Nope. Throat slit ear to ear. No prints, no evidence, no leads, no suspects."

"Sounds like Lucas to me," said Jim.

"You know, I was just thinking the same thing. Do you feel like driving north?"

"Let's go! Do you think they might really be there?"

"It's just a hunch. I could be wrong."

"You could be right. We'll never know until we get there."

Both men slightly shrugged as they hurriedly left the diner and began the long drive. Neither man mentioned it, but they both knew if they were wrong, Morgan would undoubtedly be dead by the time they returned to Georgia. Additionally, Robert was fairly certain his business was ruined, and he was wondering what in the world he was going to do to earn a living. All this was one hell of a mess, and no one playing the game seemed to know why.

Frank somehow managed to get up from the sofa without waking Morgan. He stood and stretched. He would've loved to go to sleep, but realizing Lucas could arrive at any time, Frank could not allow himself the luxury of rest. Frank found himself wandering around the cabin, trying to figure out how Lucas would attack. He also realized he was more than a little curious as to why Lucas wanted Morgan so badly that he had committed so many errors. It would have been much easier for Lucas to just let Morgan leave town, and he could have tracked her down in a couple of months. Lucas had to think Morgan knew something that was incredibly important to him. But what? What could she know? Frank played with the logs in the fire as he wondered. Then he turned back around and looked at Morgan sleeping, curled up on the sofa like a young child.

Frank knew he was her only hope of staying alive. Again he felt a twinge of guilt. Would he have even listened to her had she not mentioned Lucas? Probably not, he realized. Probably he would have arrested her on the park bench outside the federal building in Atlanta, thrown her into a holding cell, and notified the Clarke County authorities to come and pick her up. No, he realized he would not have given her the time of day. He would have dismissed her as most likely mentally ill or on drugs or simply wasting his time, looking for attention. Probably the same reaction she would have gotten from anyone in law enforcement. Who could she possibly tell that would believe even a fourth of what she said? Frank couldn't think of anyone who would believe. Suddenly, Frank felt very sorry for Morgan. He was certain she was telling the truth as she knew it to be. He also knew she couldn't prove her story or didn't know she could. Frank was her last hope.

"What is it that you know, little lady?" he whispered as he continued playing with the logs in the fire.

Lucas stopped his car about half a mile away from the cabin. Considering the weather and road conditions, he thought he had made excellent time. Methodically, Lucas stepped out of his car and put on his winter jacket and gloves. Then he checked his revolver and strapped on his hunting knife to his belt. A small revolver was strapped on his leg, just above his ankle. He then verified he had plenty of extra bullets for both guns in his coat pockets. He retrieved a nylon rope from the trunk and secured the rope around his belt also. Satisfied he could handle any situation that might arise, Lucas took a deep breath and began walking toward the cabin.

The night was calm and still. When Lucas was not walking, the only sounds he could hear were those of the snow and ice crystals landing on the already frozen ground. The sky was overcast, but there was just enough reflection from the moon and the snow on the ground to illuminate the road. It was actually most pleasant. Lucas mused at the idea that after he had killed Frank and gotten some other things under control, he might return here someday and buy the cabin. It would be a great place to relax, and as he recalled, the fishing had been fantastic down at the lake. Lucas smiled. He might just do that. He liked it here.

"It's thin, buddy," Jim said to Robert as the two sped up the highway.

"You have any better ideas?"

"Nope. Your idea makes sense, but we're never gonna get a conviction on our theory."

"I'm not in the least worried about getting a conviction," said Robert.

"Then why are we going up here?"

"Because Morgan needs some serious help, and I need some serious answers from Lucas."

The two men had worked out a fairly reasonable theory. Obviously, they could not prove a bit of it, but it was plausible. Presumably, Lucas was perhaps involved in providing cover for some major drug-running scheme. When Frank Sr. had come into town, he had notified John Henson as a professional courtesy that the FBI had an ongoing investigation, which involved the small town of Williamstown. John, as chief of police, was entitled to know. John would have immediately passed this information on to Lucas. Whether this would have happened because Lucas had been mentioned or because it was good small-town gossip, they could only guess.

As soon as Lucas had known the FBI was involved, he would have had no choice but to take some type of drastic action. Probably, Lucas had invited John to join the scheme. Lucas and John had then most likely "helped" Frank Sr. with his investigation by providing all types of inaccurate information. Eventually, as Frank Sr. had gotten too close to the truth, either Lucas or John or both had murdered the man. Either one of them would have been capable of committing the crime.

Probably, Robert figured, John had sometime later confided in Morgan about the drug deals and possibly the murder. This would have infuriated Lucas. John's blatant betrayal would have been enough reason for Lucas to kill John. Whatever information Morgan had would be enough reason for Lucas to kill Morgan.

"What are we going to do when we get there, Robert?" asked Jim.

"I really don't know. Maybe Lucas will fold when he's directly confronted. He's in a lot of trouble."

"A cornered animal usually fights," said Jim.

"I know."

The two men drove on in silence. The only sound noticeable was the windshield wipers dusting the snowflakes from the car window.

Lucas stood just outside the illumination of the security light positioned on the roof of the cabin. He knew Frank and Morgan were in there. He had seen the remnants of their footprints climbing up the driveway. Despite himself, Lucas felt very aroused. He couldn't remember being this excited about killing someone in years. Usually, it was just business, but Morgan had made this personal. This was all her fault. Yes, Lucas would cherish her death. All he needed to do now was decide on the best method of entering the cabin. The rest was bound to be easy. Lucas decided to circle around to the back of the cabin. He thought he remembered the back door had a simple old-fashioned dead bolt. If no one had changed the lock, it would be ever so easy for Lucas to pick the lock and enter the cabin. *Funny,* mused Lucas, *that an FBI agent would have a vacation home so easily accessible by an intruder. Maybe Frank Sr. had thought he was immune to an intrusion.*

Morgan continued to lie on the sofa. She really wasn't asleep, hadn't even dozed off, but she was so tired she just couldn't face any more questions from Frank. She was, however, furious still that Frank had brought her to the one place Lucas would be sure to find them. This seemed like an incredibly stupid plan to Morgan. All she wanted to do was go to her children and go away with them. She had no idea to where but just somewhere far away from Georgia. She had no idea what else she could do at the moment, so she did nothing. She lay motionless on the sofa, pretending to be asleep and wondering what in the world would happen next. She could hear Frank stirring the fire but, not feeling up for another discussion, opted to continue as she was. She began silently praying for God to give her some sort of guidance because she was all out of ideas.

Frank felt Lucas's presence more so than he actually heard the faint click of the lock from the kitchen. Frank could have easily assumed the sound came from the crackling of the fire, but he just "knew" Lucas was there. His time had come.

Lucas had quietly climbed the steps to the back door of the cabin. It still looked the same as the last time Lucas had been there. Removing a tiny penlight and a small lockpick from his jacket, only seconds passed before Lucas had the door open. Lucas drew his revolver and quietly opened the door wide enough for him to enter.

Frank, upon hearing the clicking sound, had grabbed his gun and slowly worked his way into the kitchen area. He ducked behind the small island in the kitchen so Lucas would not be able to see his shadow. Frank crouched behind the counter as he watched Lucas walk past the island.

Lucas stood in the doorway that separated the kitchen and living room areas. He had an unobstructed view of Morgan, lying motionless on the sofa. Again, Lucas was almost consumed with excitement at the thought of killing her. He had to remind himself to concentrate on the task at hand and not to get emotionally involved. "Be a professional," he said silently.

Lucas quietly inspected the room. Everything seemed to be exactly as it was the last time he had been there. He could plainly see Morgan, but where was Frank? *Surely, he wasn't sleeping,* mused Lucas. That would be too easy. Lucas would just slit Frank's throat, as he had his father's, and then all he would have left to do was to have a little conversation with Morgan and find out what she knew exactly. And then he would get rid of her. Simple. Simple plans were always the best.

Frank crawled around the island, so he was positioned behind Lucas. Frank was immediately consumed with rage, wanting nothing less than to shoot Lucas in the back of the head. Frank raised his gun, placing the barrel at the base of Lucas's skull. At the same time, Frank reached around to Lucas's hand and removed the gun Lucas was holding. "Hello, Lucas. We've been expecting you," said Frank.

Lucas, being Lucas, just laughed.

Morgan heard Lucas laugh. Never in her life had she felt such a myriad of emotions. Just the sound of Lucas laughing horrified her. She felt like she was falling, spiraling downward, falling helplessly with no way to stop. She immediately broke out into a cold sweat and felt frozen, unable to do anything more other than sit up on the sofa. She wanted to run, but she couldn't even move.

"Lucas, spread out against the wall," Frank instructed.

Lucas, though, ignored Frank and chose to speak directly to Morgan instead.

"Hello, Morgan. You've been quite exciting. I don't think I gave you enough credit. John may have been right about you."

Frank shoved Lucas in the back so that his chest was against the kitchen wall.

"Morgan," said Frank. "Get up off the sofa and go stand by the front door, please."

"Hey, Morgan," said Lucas. "I always wondered what you saw in John. Did you like being in bed with him? He was nothing. Just a small-town cop." Lucas kept on laughing.

"Shut up, Lucas, or I swear I'll kill you right now!" said Frank.

"No, you won't. Your daddy didn't, and you won't either. Such men of honor you are!" Lucas almost snickered while speaking. His eyes were locked on Morgan, but his comments were directed to Frank.

Frank almost shot Lucas at that very moment. Frank had never in his life felt such rage and contempt for another human being. *It would be so easy,* thought Frank. He had, after all, killed several people in the line of duty. Technically, he could consider this in the line of duty as well, but Frank had never shot at anyone who hadn't first fired at him. Frank knew he couldn't afford to lose his concentration, but despite his best intentions, he could hear his father speaking to him when he was just a child. His father had told him often, "Remember, son, to be an honorable man is the best you can strive for."

Just as Frank was struggling with the decision to be honorable or not, a very dishonorable Lucas Brown spun around, hitting Frank squarely in the chest. Frank's pistol fired, not hitting either one of them. Frank hit Lucas in the mouth, but Lucas was able to catch Frank in the ear with a hard blow that momentarily staggered Frank. As Frank tried to regain his equilibrium, Lucas grabbed Frank by the head and bent him over and repeatedly kneed Frank in the head. When Lucas finally released his hold, Frank fell immediately to the ground. Lucas then repeatedly kicked Frank in the side. Frank could feel his ribs cracking but was unable to do anything to stop Lucas.

"Morgan, just run!" screamed Frank. "Get out of here!"

Morgan raced for the front door. Luckily for Frank, this distracted Lucas momentarily and was probably the only reason Lucas didn't kill Frank on the spot. Instead, as Morgan struggled to unlock the front door and get out of the cabin, Lucas stopped kicking Frank and began to methodically tie him up. Morgan ran out of the front door and slipped while trying to run down the stairs. Naturally, she landed on her already injured wrist, and she screamed in pain as she did so. She got up, though, and ran through the darkness into the trees.

Morgan kept running until she couldn't catch her breath. She stopped and leaned up against a tree, trying to calm down. "Just think of something stupid," she said to herself. She couldn't think of anything stupid, and she couldn't think of anything to do. Then she heard Lucas's voice. She couldn't see him, but she heard him loud and clear.

"C'mon, Morgan. Let's go back inside. I just want to talk to you. I won't hurt you. Look, honey. It's cold out here. Let's go sit by the fire, drink some coffee, and talk this out. I have no idea why you are so scared of me. I have never hurt you."

Morgan started to run again. Lucas heard her footsteps and started laughing again.

"Morgan, you can't get away. I can see your footprints in the snow. I know you're hurt. I heard you scream when you fell. There's nowhere for you to go."

Morgan stopped running and leaned against a pine tree.

"There's nowhere for you to go." She heard this over and over in her head. She knew it was true. She couldn't hide, and there was really nowhere to go. She didn't even know where she was. Just like a deer standing in the middle of the road, frozen by the headlights of an oncoming car, Morgan just stood there, silent tears streaming down her cheeks, until Lucas caught up with her.

As she watched Lucas getting closer, Morgan could see his smile. He was always so sure of himself—the unstoppable Lucas Brown. Maybe he really was. Morgan thought he might be the devil himself. He certainly was evil enough. As Lucas reached out for her, Morgan thought she could see a small trickle of blood trailing down his chin from his bottom lip. She wouldn't remember that Lucas slapped her. She was thinking about other things.

Morgan had been eight or nine years old at the time. A horrible storm had arrived. Morgan wasn't supposed to be where she was, but she was trapped in her tree house, unable to run home because of all the rain, thunder, and lightning. Suddenly, the wind had become tremendously strong. Hail began falling from the sky, bouncing haphazardly off the tree house. Morgan had stood motionless, looking out of the tree house window.

Her mouth had dropped open as she saw the funnel cloud descend from the sky. She never moved as the tornado tore a path headed directly toward her. She was fascinated. She knew she was in danger, knew her parents were going to be incredibly angry with her when, and if, she ever got home. And still, she just stood there. The tornado was less than fifty yards away from the tree house when it mercifully climbed back into the sky.

Somehow, that had all worked out all right. Her parents had even been so happy to see her safe. They hadn't even spanked her for being outside when she knew she shouldn't have been.

Morgan would have given anything in the world if she could have gone back to that tree house at this particular moment. She had always thought of it as her safe place. Morgan was having a difficult time, though, imagining a scenario where her current situation would turn out as well as the tornado incident. This wasn't shaping up to be a "happily ever after" type of story.

CHAPTER 23

Harry Sprewell was livid. The initial searches of Lucas's home and office had not turned up any useful information or evidence. He still did not even have a true idea of what was really going on. All he knew for sure was that one of his best agents, Frank, was missing. Presumably, Morgan was with Frank; therefore, she was missing as well. Lucas may have been looking for them, or he may have gone into hiding. Maybe Frank was dead. Maybe Morgan was dead. Who knew? Probably, Daniel Jacobs knew, but he couldn't very well tell anyone since he had blown off his head. People from the justice department were calling, demanding answers, but they weren't answering any questions either.

Harry turned to one of his aides. "Go pick up Robert and Jim. Apologize for waking them, but get them back here quickly. We're running out of time."

"Yes, sir," the aide replied, grateful to be able to leave the room.

"How far away are we?" Robert asked Jim. He was getting angrier by the minute and wanted nothing but to confront Lucas.

"Probably two or three more hours, depending on the weather," answered Jim.

"Damn it! This is taking too long!"

"Man, you don't even know if they are there. We could be wrong, you know."

"We're not wrong. I know we're not."

Just as the moon was going down, trying to give way to the dawn, the agent dispatched to retrieve Robert and Jim called Harry. "I cannot find them, sir."

"What do you mean you can't find them?"

"I've been to both residences and the business office and the hospital. They just aren't here."

The length of Harry's tirade that followed would be memorable. Immediately, the agent on the phone and all the agents in the room with Harry knew something big was happening. They all wondered why they hadn't been briefed. They had no way of knowing their leader, Harry, had no idea himself. Harry did know, however, that some big shot from the CIA was on his way from Washington. And Harry did not yet have anything to tell him.

Morgan regained consciousness back in the cabin. She was sitting in a chair, her hands tied behind her. Frank was tied in a chair beside her in a similar fashion. Morgan looked at Frank and felt as if she would vomit. His eyes were so swollen he only had tiny slits through which to see, and each time he took a breath, his face contorted with pain. Morgan could hear pots and pans clanging in the kitchen. She could hear Lucas humming, presumably as he cooked.

"Well," Morgan whispered to Frank, "this was certainly a fantastic idea."

"This really isn't the right time for you to be a smart-ass, Morgan" was Frank's reply.

"Really? Honestly, it seems like a damn good time to me. Any more bright ideas?"

"Not yet, but I'm working on a few." And Frank actually smiled at her.

Morgan realized, though, that it was a smile of pity. They were in a big mess. Morgan was furious at herself for being so useless, and Frank was furious at himself for having let his guard down, however briefly. A lapse of only a couple of seconds would now most likely cost them their lives. Frank had let Morgan down. He knew his father would have been disappointed also.

The only good part of Frank's current shame and humiliation was that it somewhat dulled the pain he was feeling. He had no idea how to fight Lucas now, but he knew he was going to die trying.

Lucas emerged from the kitchen, sliding a small dinette table in front of him. "It's a great day for a good, hearty breakfast, don't you think?" He was smiling, and Morgan felt a hatred for Lucas she wasn't aware she was capable of feeling.

Neither Frank nor Morgan answered. Morgan thought this had to be the surreal scene she would ever witness. Here they were, Frank and Morgan, tied to chairs in front of a fireplace. Frank was obviously badly hurt, and Lucas was setting up a kitchen table in the living room to have his breakfast in front of them. Momentarily, Morgan thought she might be hallucinating or dreaming. It couldn't be real. No way.

Lucas, however, continued to set his table. Shortly, he emerged from the kitchen with a glass of orange juice and a cup of coffee. Continuing to hum, he walked back into the kitchen and came back with a plate of bacon and eggs, toast and grits. He seemed quite pleased with himself. Lucas raised his cup of coffee in a fake toast to Frank and Morgan as he began eating his breakfast.

"You know," Lucas said, "I'd love to invite you two to join me, but so far, you two have been most ungracious as hosts." Lucas smiled, and Morgan knew without a doubt that Lucas was the evilest person she had ever encountered.

Morgan continued to sit there, not that she had any choice in the matter, and watched Lucas in total disbelief as he calmly ate his breakfast. She felt as if she was not there, rather someone standing back, watching as the plot to a movie began to unfold. She was fairly certain she wasn't going to like the final scene. Nope, there wasn't going to be a happy ending this time.

Lucas appeared to be calm, but in the back of his mind, he kept hearing the last words John had told him, "She knows just about everything."

"So, Morgan," said Lucas, "why don't you tell me everything John told you, and we can all go home, OK?"

"John didn't tell me anything that would interest you, Lucas. We talked about things lovers talk about. Nothing else."

She knows just about everything.

"Lucas, I can assure you, she knows nothing that you need to know," said Frank. "I've been talking to her for three days, and she is really totally clueless."

"No she is not!" Lucas snapped back and shoved a piece of bacon in his mouth, glaring at Morgan while he chewed.

She knows just about everything.

"Lucas, listen to me," implored Frank. "I know you killed my dad. I know it was you who killed John because Morgan was with me at the time of his death. We can't prove any of that, and you know it. All you need to do is leave. You can get away with it all. You can't be tied to anything."

Frank was trying to reason with Lucas, but it was extremely difficult for him to talk. His ribs ached, along with his head, and breathing was becoming a major challenge. Anyway, how exactly does one successfully reason with a madman? Frank assumed most or any hostage negotiator would have a difficult time with Lucas. After all, Lucas had more training than some of the most experienced negotiators.

"Morgan, I'm giving you one more chance." Lucas had finished his meal and was sipping his coffee and leaning back in the chair. "First," he said, "you'll tell me every little detail John whispered to you when you were in bed together. Then you're going to tell me anything and everything else you know. Then we'll go get your kids and see what happens after that."

"You will not touch my kids, Lucas," said Morgan.

"Sure, I will, Morgan. I know where they are. I know what they had for dinner last night. The only question left is whether or not you get to see them again. They might be at the end of the driveway for all you know."

Morgan prayed he was bluffing. It had to be a bluff. She looked desperately at Lucas's eyes to see if she could tell. She couldn't. Lucas had the same expression John used to have when he wasn't going to tell her something she wanted to know. *They must train these guys for this,* she thought. Morgan's head was swimming. Lucas couldn't have found her children. Frank and the entire FBI hadn't found them, so how could Lucas? But Lucas always seemed to come out on top. Maybe he did have them. Maybe he had already killed them. Maybe, just as in her dream, Lucas had slit their throats as they had slept. It would be the same other than it was Lucas killing them instead of John. Maybe the dream had been more of a premonition than a nightmare. Morgan felt more lost than ever. She didn't know what to say or even what to think. She glanced over at Frank, but he didn't say anything. Then miraculously, Morgan calmed down. She realized if Lucas did have her daughters, there was no point in doing or saying anything. They would all be dead soon anyway. There wasn't going to be a happy ending, and they wouldn't be going home together. What did it really matter then?

"Lucas," she said, "I will tell you everything just as soon as I see my girls."

The men from Washington had arrived in Clarkston. Harry Sprewell was ordered to turn over all the information they had gathered to them. Harry was told he was no longer needed and they were assuming jurisdiction in the matter.

"And just who are you to claim jurisdiction?" asked Harry.

"We're from Washington. That's all you need to know."

"Until I see some identification or some written official orders, you don't get anything. I've got a missing agent, a girl wanted for a murder she didn't commit, missing kids, dead people all over the state, and Lucas Brown is nowhere to be found."

"We only want Brown. You can have the rest of the mess. Where is he?"

"I just told you. He is nowhere to be found."

"Let's take a look at what you have, and we'll decide after that."

The two men sat down at the table in the hotel room and began poring over every piece of information they had collected. Of course, they had the same information Robert and Jim had, but not one of them picked up on the connection between Frank's father and John Henson. After all, Frank Haggerty Sr. was a senior FBI agent who routinely traveled all across the Southeast, investigating tips and rumors. It wasn't considered strange that he had once come to this small town in Georgia.

The nameless man from Washington claimed to be with the CIA although he offered no such proof. He did, however, seem convinced that Daniel Jacobs could have explained everything had he not blown his brains out while under the supervision of the FBI. This little jab was not lost on Harry, but he chose to ignore the comment. He still didn't know who this man was. The man from Washington didn't come up with any answers either.

Robert and Jim had managed to get within twenty miles of the cabin. The sun had started to finally rise, but the road conditions were terrible. The two men were listening to the police scanner when they heard they were being looked for too. Since they had unexpectedly disappeared, it was a possibility they could be assisting Lucas.

"Man," said Robert. Thirty years in law enforcement and tons of commendations and awards and now he was possibly assisting his former business partner in numerous criminal acts. Thirty years down the drain because of his former best friend, and Robert still didn't know why.

"We're in a lot of trouble here," said Jim.

"Yeah, I guess we are," said Robert.

The two men reached an intersection.

"Which way do I turn?" asked Jim.

"Take a right, I think."

If they had gone to the left, they would have been at the cabin in less than half an hour. Unfortunately, with the snowstorm, some of the roads had been closed and detour signs were set up. The particular detour sign at this unmarked intersection had been blown over during the night. A little more than an hour from now, the two men would find themselves stuck in a snowdrift on a closed mountain road. Of course, they didn't have any way of knowing this at this time.

CHAPTER 24

Lucas got up and walked around the sofa and knelt in front of Morgan. She wanted nothing more than to kick him, but she couldn't as he had tied her ankles to the legs of the chair.

"Let me explain something to you, dear," Lucas said. "You don't make any requests or demands here. I ask the questions, and you answer them. You've caused me a lot of trouble."

Lucas had spent years training for difficult situations. He had faced death dozens of times, and never had he lost his concentration or let fear get the best of him. This situation was proving to be different—maybe because he was being ostracized by his employer or maybe because Morgan had created such a mess, he didn't know. Lucas did know his head was spinning, and despite himself and his training, he was struggling to remain calm.

She knows just about everything.

a-b-o-r-t

You, Lucas, have created a huge mess.

Do not call here again. You are on your own.

Morgan noticed Lucas was perspiring ever so lightly on his upper lip. He had to be nervous. It surely wasn't warm enough in the cabin to sweat. Somehow, this helped to calm Morgan too. She said nothing, choosing instead to simply stare at Lucas.

Lucas raised his hand to Morgan's face. He cupped her face with his hand and squeezed until it became painful.

"I will not ask you again," Lucas hissed.

"My daughters have a letter with them, and if I don't show up by tomorrow, the letter goes to the press. You will be finished, Lucas" was her reply.

Frank laughed. He knew not to, but dang, Morgan was spunky. He even found himself wondering if it might be true. What would she have written in the letter? Who would have paid any attention to such a crazy story even if she had?

Ever so briefly, a cloud passed across Lucas's face. Morgan saw it, just as Frank did. How had that bothered him? Morgan finally decided Lucas needed to know something John had known.

Lucas untied Morgan's right wrist. He had tied it tightly, and it had hurt as it was the wrist she had cracked when jumping into the swimming pool and landed on when falling down the stairs. Lucas gently stroked her fingers.

"Morgan," he said, "I don't have time for any of your crap. I don't find you cute like John did, and personally, I think you're a pain in the butt."

Finishing his sentence, Lucas firmly grabbed her wrist and twisted it so hard he could hear the bones separate in her wrist. Morgan screamed in pain. Frank would have killed Lucas at that moment if he had the opportunity.

"Listen, Lucas," said Frank. "The FBI will be here in a matter of minutes. It's over. Let it go. Another murder isn't going to help you any."

Lucas replied, "I don't imagine another murder or two would hurt anything either."

When Morgan could speak again, she looked at Lucas. "I need to lie down, please. I'm going to pass out if I don't, and if I pass out, I can't tell you anything."

Lucas thought about the request. He couldn't care less about her comfort and actually hoped he had hurt her enough for her to pass out. But even though he didn't believe Frank's story about the FBI being on the way, Lucas possibly needed to get this over with and be on his way. Lucas untied Morgan from the chair and roughly shoved her on the sofa.

Morgan curled up into a ball, trying to make herself seem small. Lucas mused at how weak and stupid she was.

Robert and Jim were trying to take a curve as quickly as they could. A sense of urgency had built up between them as the sun had come up. Somehow, the stakes seemed much higher now. As they rounded the corner, they slid off the road and ran into the snowbank. It wasn't anyone's fault. There wasn't anywhere for them to go. That was why the road, with the blown-over detour sign, had been closed.

"Where's the damn cabin?" yelled Robert as he jumped out of the car.

"It should be due north of here. I don't know if we can get there or not," said Jim.

"We'll hike it. It's sure got to be quicker than this."

The two men grabbed their jackets from the car. Then they grabbed their revolvers from the glove box and began hiking up the mountain through the trees. Both felt they did not have the time to backtrack along the road.

Lucas was getting more agitated. He was ready for all this to end. He knew he needed to get moving, and he was tired of waiting on Morgan to tell him anything useful. He walked into the kitchen to get some water.

"Morgan, listen to me," whispered Frank. "If you get the chance, jump over the sofa and lunge for the desk. There's a gun in the top drawer. If you get the gun, honey, just shoot him. Don't think about it, just pull the trigger."

"Frank, I don't think I could pull the trigger right now." She was telling the truth. Morgan couldn't even feel her fingers, much less move them. She hated herself for being weak and helpless, but there didn't seem to be anything else she could do about it.

"Just grab it with your left hand, point, and pull the trigger. We're running out of options here, honey."

"Really? I hadn't noticed," she replied with fake surprise.

Frank looked at her with disapproval but decided to remain silent.

Lucas could hear his two captives whispering, and though he couldn't make out what they were saying, he could see them. No one was trying to move, so there wasn't any problem. Only the voices in

Lucas's head continued to distract him. Try as he might, Lucas could not silence the voices.

She knows just about everything.

You've made quite a mess, Lucas.

a-b-o-r-t... a-b-o-r-t... a-b-o-r-t

We can't help you now.

Over and over again, Lucas heard them. Even when he was speaking, he could still hear the voices. Lucas Brown would not fail. Lucas Brown could not fail. He had never failed at anything in his life, and he didn't intend to now. He was worried, though, that he could be running out of time. Lucas decided he would just lay out the truth and see if he could find the kids and kill them all. He was through being calm and waiting. He had other things to do. Lucas Brown was a very busy man.

Lucas walked out of the kitchen, a glass of water in his hand. He walked behind Frank and stirred the fire. *No reason for them to be cold, not at least until they were dead,* mused Lucas.

"All right. Here's how this is going to go," said Lucas. "I'm going to tell you everything, and you're going to tell me what's in the letter, assuming there really is one."

"You must think there is, or you wouldn't be talking about it," mumbled Morgan.

"Shut up! I am so very tired of you! Just lie there and listen because when I am finished, you are dead. Do you understand?"

Morgan nodded. She really hoped it would be a long story. She wasn't in any great hurry to die.

"Once upon a time, our great government had some balls. Presidencies were bought and paid for, just like one buys a business. The highest bidder would win. Naturally, certain people who guaranteed election results expected to be paid. They also paid certain other people quite nicely to ensure they would be paid."

"You mean the Mafia, right?" asked Morgan.

"Sometimes. Anyway, the CIA used to be an agency by itself. It didn't have to answer to anyone. All they had to do was keep the country safe, and it didn't matter how they did it. No big deal. But then here comes the Kennedys. Their old man—he understood. He bought the position and agreed to pay the price. Not JFK though. He thought he didn't have to answer to anyone. He made his own rules.

"They tried to warn him, but he wouldn't listen. He thought he was so much better than everyone else. So long story short, we killed him. The United States of America murdered its own president. Unfortunately, everyone in the CIA at the time knew what had happened, as well as a few young soldiers."

Morgan and Frank listened, mostly in disbelief. Lucas recited his story as if it were a fairy tale. Nothing wrong with any of it. Just the way things were.

"Naturally," Lucas continued, "the ramifications of such a decision were tremendous. The idiotic American public went crazy. Hell, they still love the Kennedys. Jackie knew the truth. Now she was a lady. She figured out to go on with her life and just let go. Eventually, things died down a bit. And then all of a sudden, the CIA gets wind of a couple of retirees running off at the mouth about what happened. That's where I come in."

Lucas paused to see if Morgan was going to say anything. She didn't, so he continued. "Obviously, the Americans would never be able to accept what happened. There would be absolute anarchy. And the press! The self-righteous, entitled press comes along and declares they have the right to know everything with the stupid Freedom of Information Act. This cannot happen. So a small elite group was formed, which I have had the great honor to supervise. Most of the men who were still alive were set up in Clarke County in various positions to simply live out their lives. All they had to do was just not say anything.

"For some reason, some men, as they grow older, feel the need to cleanse their souls. They start drinking. They start talking. Usually, no one pays any attention to them. But once they say too much, they have to be eliminated for obvious reasons. A car wreck, a suicide, whatever could conveniently look like a tragic accident—we've done it for years, and we will continue to do so. The American people could never accept the truth."

Frank didn't know what to say. He assumed his father had either been offered a job from Lucas or discovered what Lucas was doing. Either way, Frank knew his father would have never agreed to such a situation. At least Frank now knew why his father had been killed. Small consolation as it was, but sometimes, an answer is all one can hope for.

"Lucas, what makes you think I even care?" asked Morgan. "Personally, I think you and John are insane. All I wanted to do was get away from you both."

"But he told you, didn't he?" asked Lucas.

"Sure, he did, and I wrote it all down in the letter that is with my daughters. If you let me go, I'll disappear and destroy the letter. And no one will ever know. Like I said, I couldn't care less."

"You have to care, Morgan," sneered Lucas. "This is about our country—the greatest country in the world. Do you realize this becoming public knowledge would do more damage to America than the 9/11 attacks? America has someone to blame for that, someone to hate. If this ever became public knowledge, it would absolutely destroy our country. You, as stupid as you are, could ruin the greatest nation in the history of the world." Lucas almost spit at her as he spoke. He couldn't fathom the situation had come to this. This was insanity.

Robert and Jim crested the top of another incline. As they did, they saw Lucas's Jeep Wrangler.

"We were right!" said Jim.

"Yeah," said Robert. "I just hope we're not too late."

"I don't think so, or he'd be gone. He's got to know a lot of people are looking for him."

"Let's get going," said Robert, and the two men almost ran to the driveway of the cabin.

As the cabin came into view, the men quickly formed their strategy. Jim would go around to the back of the cabin, and Robert would enter through the front door. Robert would give Jim five minutes to work his way around to the back door, and then simultaneously, both men would enter the cabin.

"Be careful" was the last thing Robert would ever say to Jim.

Oddly enough, Lucas felt pretty good. It felt great to actually tell someone how important he had been to the United States of America. He knew Frank and Morgan couldn't grasp the importance of what he had told them, but it felt good all the same. He excused himself to go to the restroom.

The situation was, of course, much more complicated than someone like Morgan could have ever understood, and Lucas didn't have any intention of trying to explain it to her. Just the implication that the United States of America had murdered their own president would reduce this great country to the same level as some of the Third World countries the United States regularly stepped in to help control.

Should the public ever really know what happened, sheer anarchy would reign. The government would not have any credibility. Possibly, when all was said and done, the government might not even exist. The balance of power would shift, and it was impossible to predict how all that might turn out. The ramifications were endless.

"Now, Morgan!" whispered Frank as Lucas walked out of the room.

Morgan slid over behind the sofa and even managed to get the gun from the desk drawer, but as she did so, she was so dizzy she couldn't even see clearly enough to try to find Lucas to try to shoot him. She slid back over the sofa just as Lucas emerged back into the room.

Lucas walked back over to the table where he had consumed his breakfast. His revolver was lying on the table, and he raised it and pointed it at Frank.

"Now, darling," Lucas said, "you will tell me exactly what I want to know. If you don't, I will blow your friend's freaking head off."

"Lucas, please leave Frank alone. Get me out of here, and I'll take you to the girls. But only if you let him go."

"Are you sleeping with him now too? I told John you were nothing but a tramp. He wouldn't listen, though. He had quite a thing for you.

You're the reason all of this happened. A stupid little tramp like you. Hard to believe, isn't it?"

"Yeah, Lucas. It's real hard to believe," said Frank, trying to distract him. He prayed Morgan would try to shoot Lucas, but Frank didn't see her even trying to move.

The problem wasn't that Morgan didn't want to shoot Lucas. She would have gladly done so at that particular moment. She just didn't think she could maneuver around quickly enough and aim the gun at him and hit him with her left hand. Every time she moved, she felt she was going to vomit. She wasn't even sure she would remain conscious long enough to make that many moves. The only thing Morgan was certain of was that they were about to die. She wished she was braver, wished she was stronger.

Morgan thought about her daughters. She wondered where they would end up. Who would take care of them? She could see them running toward her, waving and saying, "Hi, Mommy!" She wanted to cry. She wanted to hug them. She wanted to go away. She just wanted it all over.

"Tell me where the letter is, Morgan," said Lucas.

"Go to hell, Lucas," she said, certain it would be the last thing she would say.

Lucas turned and fired his revolver, hitting Morgan squarely in the right shoulder. The pain was incredible, but all she could think was she didn't know why he just didn't cut her whole right arm off. Instinctively, Morgan tried to slow the bleeding from her shoulder with her left hand. Everything was going dark for her, and she knew she was going to bleed to death.

Robert and Jim both heard the shot. They still had a little more than a minute before they were supposed to enter the cabin. Robert prayed that Jim was thinking the same thing as he crept onto the porch. "We've got to go now, buddy," whispered Robert as he readied himself to bust down the door. Jim was on the back steps, wishing for the same thing.

Lucas turned toward Frank, the pistol aimed between Frank's eyes.

"You can't cover this up, Lucas," said Frank. "There's been too much killing. You got sloppy. Even if you kill us, they will catch you. Do you have any idea how many people are looking for you now?"

"I don't care. I'll get rid of you two, find the kids, kill them, and disappear. Nothing to it. Time to go. Try to die with the same dignity your father did, Frank." Lucas pulled back the hammer on the revolver.

Morgan tried to reach her gun but couldn't. Then miraculously, there was a banging sound from the front of the cabin. This bang was immediately followed by another from somewhere around the kitchen. Morgan held her breath. Lucas jerked around, trying to figure out what was happening. Simultaneously, Robert burst in through the front door and Jim emerged from the back door, entering the cabin through the kitchen. Frank tipped his chair over, throwing his tied hands into the fireplace.

"Lucas, freeze!" yelled Robert, revolver aimed at Lucas.

Lucas, surprised as he was to see Robert, knew Robert would never shoot him. They had been friends for years. As Lucas turned toward the noise in the kitchen, though, he saw Jim. He knew Jim would shoot. Lucas fired at Jim. Jim fired at Lucas. Robert ducked behind the door and tried, unsuccessfully, to get a clear shot at Lucas.

Frank, thrusting his hands and arms into the fireplace, burned the ropes away from his hands. His feet were still tied to the chair, and his hands were badly burned. But there wasn't any time to worry about that. "Morgan, toss me the gun!"

Morgan rolled over, grabbed the gun with her left hand, and threw with all the strength she had left. It was a perfect throw. *Fine time to finally get something right,* Morgan thought to herself. Frank caught the gun, aimed, and shot Lucas in the head.

Lucas was spinning around after firing his gun at Jim, trying to determine who fired the last shot he heard. The bullet from Frank's gun caught Lucas directly in his right temple. Lucas didn't have a chance to react. Immediately, his eyes seemed blinded by a bright white flash. As the bullet pierced his skull, his eardrum burst, followed instantly by parts of his brain being torn apart. The bullet exited above his left eye socket, but half of Lucas's head separated with the bullet's departure, so the exit wound would be difficult to find.

The image of Lucas's blown-away face would haunt Morgan for years. Robert emerged from the front door, gun drawn, trying to evaluate the situation. Lucas was dead. Jim was dying, bleeding to death, lying face down in the kitchen, fatally wounded from the bullet that struck his heart.

Frank, feet still tied to the chair, was trying to get to Morgan. Morgan had a tremendous amount of blood on her, and Robert immediately had no idea if she was all right or not. Frank managed to get to Morgan and cradled her in his arms. Robert came over to the two of them, and Morgan looked up at him. "We're sure glad to see you, Robert," she said and began to cry.

"If you've got a cell phone, we need to get a helicopter up here quickly," said Frank.

"Sure thing," said Robert, and he called Harry Sprewell.

As Robert was calling Sprewell, a number of things began to happen. Immediately, helicopters were sent to pick up the three survivors. Harry and the men from Washington were immediately en route to a small cabin in the North Carolina mountains.

Morgan was about to pass out on Frank. She had lost a great deal of blood, not to mention, the trauma. And Frank was immensely concerned as to whether or not she was going to survive. He didn't think her chances were very good. "Morgan, honey, listen to me. Where are your kids? Lucas's dead. You've got to trust me. Where are they?" Frank almost shook her as he asked the question.

"Disney World" was the faint answer.

"Where, honey?"

"They are at Disney World. I figured they might as well have a good time. They've got to be out of money, though." Morgan smiled as she said all this.

Frank, totally surprised, laughed and relayed the message to Robert.

Another helicopter was dispatched to Orlando, Florida, to get the girls. The last thing Morgan remembered was Frank gently shaking her, telling her not to say anything about what had happened until she talked to him.

"Do you understand, honey?"

Morgan nodded. She didn't have anything left to say, but oddly enough, her thoughts were quite clear. She was at the end of her plan and had no idea what would happen next. She didn't have any clue what she was going to do, but she did know one thing. She damn sure trusted Frank, and if he said don't talk to anyone, that was exactly what she was going to do.

CHAPTER 25

Two days later, Morgan woke up in the hospital with her oldest daughter tapping her on the face. "Wake up, Mommy. Mommy, wake up!"

It was the sweetest thing she had ever heard in her life. She opened her eyes and saw both daughters standing on chairs beside her bed. She began to cry as she hugged them both with her left arm. Naturally, they climbed on top of her, hitting her right arm. But she couldn't have cared less.

Morgan's cousin, the one who Lucas hadn't been able to find, had taken the girls to Disney World at Morgan's instructions. However, she was thoroughly confused and a bit agitated about the recent events. "What have you gotten yourself into?" she asked as Morgan was hugging the girls.

"It doesn't matter. It's over now," said Morgan.

"It does matter. My god! You send us off to Disney, tell me to stay there until you call. You didn't call. I almost lost my job. And then a helicopter lands in the hotel parking lot, and we're whisked off here and guarded around the clock. I do think an explanation would be appropriate!"

The guards outside the door heard the cousin raising her voice, and she was politely escorted from the hospital. Morgan couldn't help but smile. She knew her cousin had no idea what had happened, but it was funny all the same. Someday, a long time from now, she would call her cousin and try to give her an explanation. Morgan had no idea what the explanation would be, but she would have time to worry about that later.

Morgan was heavily sedated, so her daughters were not allowed to stay long. They, too, were escorted from the hospital to a nearby hotel where they had the best babysitters the United States government could employ. The girls were having a grand time. Morgan found it quite amusing.

Frank entered her room a few minutes later. "Hey, honey, how are you feeling?" he asked.

Morgan looked at him. His face was badly bruised, and his hands were bandaged. Slowly, she was remembering all that had happened even though she really didn't cherish the memory. "What exactly happened?" she asked.

"Lucas's dead. A lot of people want to talk to you. Do you remember what I told you before we left the cabin?"

Morgan nodded. She remembered no one had arrived before Lucas had told his tale. She correctly assumed this was what Frank was talking about.

"Just leave everything to me, honey. It's all going to be fine. Get some sleep."

Frank left the hospital, and as he drove to his hotel for the night, he reflected on everything that had occurred. He wished he could understand why he had done what he did, why he had risked everything to help a troubled young woman he didn't know. Maybe it was because he had daughters of his own. Maybe it was because after he lost his wife and family, he had given up on being happy. Maybe he was tired of working for the bureau. Maybe he wanted revenge for his father's death. Maybe he had been a lost soul with no purpose. Maybe helping Morgan, even though he had no reason to do so, would be his chance at redemption.

Frank had always tried to be a good man and had always tried to do the right thing as long as it was legal. His wife divorced him shortly after his father was murdered, and Frank had become very withdrawn and depressed. He didn't tell anyone how he felt, but Frank blamed

God for all of it. There couldn't be any other reason. His father didn't deserve to die that way. His wife couldn't have had any real reason for leaving him. Not having any other answers, Frank blamed the only one he could think of—God. But with Lucas dead—and surprisingly, Frank felt no joy in killing him—and Morgan finally safe, Frank was once again at peace.

Now suddenly, Frank understood it all. He remembered driving to the bar, struggling with his decision to carry out an illegal act. Frank had muttered "God, help me" even though he hadn't expected any help. But he knew he had had help. There was no other way it could have happened. Morgan would have never been able to toss the gun so perfectly, and Frank should have never been able to fire the last shot so quickly that Lucas didn't have time to respond. Frank had asked for help, and he had gotten it. Frank understood. Morgan said she owed Frank her life, but he knew he owed his soul to her. Without Morgan, Frank would have remained lost forever. Frank wondered if Morgan had any idea what she had done for him.

Morgan did sleep. Thankful for the painkillers the doctors gave her intravenously, she slept without dreams. At the time, that was the best gift she could have received. A few days later, she was removed from the hospital and taken to a suite at a hotel not far from there. A nurse was at her bedside twenty-four hours a day. Frank visited daily, along with several federal psychologists and investigators. Harry Sprewell also visited every day. Daily she was questioned on what had happened, her relationship with John, her connection with Lucas, and basically, every event in her life. Eventually, they all decided Morgan simply couldn't remember what had happened due to the entire trauma she had suffered. Morgan didn't think Harry was buying the story at all, but Frank told her to stick to her story of knowing nothing, and she did.

Robert visited a few times before returning home. Morgan thanked him profusely as they were saying goodbye. She said she was sorry Jim had died. She was sorry Lucas had had to die also. Robert simply said things had a way of working out, and he had gone.

Finally, on a day when Morgan was allowed to get out of bed, she and Frank went for a walk. They walked far ahead of the agents guarding her so no one could hear their conversation.

"You did good, lady," said Frank.

"I still don't know what I did," she answered.

"Yes, you do. Listen, in a couple of days, you're going to get to leave. Do you have anywhere to go?"

"No, I don't know who will even talk to me now."

"OK, Robert and I have a rental car for you. There's an envelope with a thousand dollars in the glove box. When you leave here, all of your things will be in the trunk. You get in the car and drive. I don't care where you go, but don't go anywhere you have ever been. My cell phone number is written on the envelope with the money. You call me if you need anything." Frank smiled at her. "It's all going to be all right."

"So how does all of this end? I really don't understand."

"Really, it's going to work out well. You can't remember anything, and I never found out anything very relevant, so we're not too important. As far as the general public is concerned, Jim and Lucas were killed while on duty. Lucas's family, though, will never collect a dime of his life insurance or pension. Jim's family will be taken care of financially. John's murder has been classified as a burglary. You've been cleared of all charges.

"Lucas's friend Daniel Jacobs committed suicide due to the continued illness of his daughter. Ricky the hit man, as you called him, had a tragic trucking accident in Georgia the day after Lucas died. A couple of guys have left Clarkston, and I understand there's all kinds of stuff going on in Washington, but you'll never know about it. I imagine a few pardons will come along in the next few weeks, and a few elected officials will retire due to personal reasons. Besides that, it's all over with. Done."

"So it's all over just like that? What about what he did? What about the lives he ruined?" Morgan was getting upset.

Frank understood, but he wanted her to understand also. "Honey, the lives that were destroyed will still be destroyed. We're talking about some major stuff here. Big stuff. If you want to talk, I'll stand behind you, but I won't be in charge. Washington is more than willing to place you in their witness protection program, but I don't think you'd like it much. You can't change what they did. You can expose it, but all you're going to do is open a can of worms. I don't think you want the fight. It would make what you went through seem like a friendly game of tag football."

"But what was it Lucas wanted with me?"

"Honey, your lover gave you a lot of details about a government conspiracy, and then you got caught in the middle of the conspiracy to cover up the conspiracy. The United States government doesn't particularly like to look that bad, and you have the knowledge to make them look like shit. But you know all that anyway."

Morgan walked in silence for a few minutes. The last thing she wanted was to talk to anyone about what had happened. She wanted a life with her daughters, a safe life with no problems. She would be happy to pretend none of it had happened. "You're right. I'll be free to go?" she asked.

"Yes. As long as you can't remember anything, nobody can expect anything from you. Understand?"

"Yes, sir. I sure do. Are you going to call your wife now?"

Frank smiled. "I already did. As soon as you're safely out of town, we're going to dinner."

"Don't forget, chase her until you catch her," Morgan said, smiling. They both laughed and headed back to the hotel room.

Three days later, Frank awakened Morgan at five in the morning. "Let's get going. Your car awaits. Your bags are in the trunk. Your medicine is in the front of the car, and you're all set."

"I'm going to miss you," she said to Frank as they rode in the elevator to the parking garage.

"Call me anytime you want to," he said, smiling.

"Thank you. That's not enough to say, but I don't know how else to say it."

"I'm not near as noble as you think, Morgan. I never would have helped you if Lucas hadn't killed my father, but I think you knew that all along anyway. Now listen to me. The rental car is yours for two weeks. When the two weeks are up, just abandon it in a parking lot somewhere. The local police will return the car to the rental company. Don't call anyone for a while unless you call me. Let all of this die down."

"I don't have any idea what I'm going to do," she said, suddenly frightened of the idea of having to start all over again. The thousand dollars was a fantastic gift, but it would hardly set the three of them up somewhere. *Oh well,* Morgan thought, *it sure as hell beat being dead.*

As they entered the parking garage, Morgan saw her daughters seated in the back of the rental car, waiting for her. The car was surrounded by no less than ten FBI agents. Morgan started laughing.

Frank stopped her as she was getting into the car. "Don't drive any farther than you can safely. You're still not well. Take care of yourself. I promise you'll be fine."

"You're one fine man, Frank," said Morgan, and she kissed him on the cheek as she got into the car. Morgan got onto the interstate and drove north. She had no idea where they were going. But she planned on driving until she needed to sleep, and then they would get a hotel room. Her daughters were so happy to finally be back with their mother that they didn't even ask when they could stop riding. The three of them sang songs and told stories for hours.

Fifteen hours, four bathroom stops, and two meals later, they stopped at a hotel for the evening. Morgan had been exhausted for several hours but wanted to get as far away as she could before she had to stop. The girls ran inside the hotel room, eager to check out the television and hopeful of going swimming before having to go to bed. Morgan opened the trunk of the car to remove the luggage and immediately saw a briefcase with an envelope taped to it. Cautiously, Morgan removed the envelope and read the enclosed letter:

Dear Morgan,

While we were waiting on the helicopters to come and get us, Robert and I had time to search Lucas's car. He seemed to have an abundance of cash. Robert and I can't take the

money as it would be highly unethical. However, if we turned it in, it would just be lost in the system. We decided, therefore, it should be your reward for your brave service to your country.
Take care.

With much love and admiration,
Robert and Frank

Opening the briefcase upon locking the hotel room, Morgan found the briefcase to contain $400,000. She was shocked and amazed and immensely grateful. She could start over now. The burden of the world was lifted from her shoulders at that moment. She sat on the bed in the hotel room and simultaneously laughed and cried.

CHAPTER 26

Thirteen days later, an abandoned rental car was discovered in a parking lot of a shopping mall in Boston, Massachusetts. Frank was notified and was satisfied that all was well with Morgan and the girls. Morgan frequently wanted to call Frank, but somehow, she managed to refrain from picking up the phone. She correctly assumed it would only further complicate matters if the two of them stayed in contact.

Three months later, Morgan was sitting by the edge of a swimming pool at a hotel in the Florida Keys. Her daughters were swimming, and she was trying to catnap as they did. A lifeguard was on duty, so she assumed they would be safe. Morgan still had trouble sleeping. Every night, she had to struggle with the memories and the nightmares. She hoped eventually they would fade away, but she really doubted they would. Until then, though, she would continue to pace the floor at night, watching over her daughters and napping during the day as she could.

Morgan had decided to settle in the Florida Keys. She liked the islands and was intending to open a small gift shop. She only wanted to earn enough to sustain a modest lifestyle for her and her daughters until she could find a farm and figure out how to run an animal rescue and not go broke. Her gift from Robert and Frank would be more than enough to allow for that.

Morgan got up from the lounge chair from which she was sitting and walked to the bar to get a drink. As she was sitting at the bar, waiting for her drink, a handsome gentleman took the seat next to her. "Hi. My name's George," he said, flashing a bright smile at her.

"Hi" was all she said.

"Listen, do you know much about the area? I just got in, and I can't find my way around here at all."

"It's not that hard. You'll get used to it." And with that, Morgan paid for her drink and went back to the pool.

Under different circumstances, she might have found him very attractive, but not nearly enough time had gone by since John had died. Despite herself, Morgan still missed the closeness she felt when she had been with him. The last thing she wanted was another relationship with someone else. *Maybe someday,* she thought. *Not now though.*

The handsome man left the bar without a drink. Walking around behind the bar, he removed his cell phone from his pants pocket and dialed a number. "She's here," he said to the unseen individual on the other end of the conversation.

"Don't let her out of your sight. We still don't know what John told her. Eventually, everybody talks."

CPSIA information can be obtained
at www.ICGtesting.com
Printed in the USA
LVOW12*1520090218

565960LV00003B/31/P